I0739765

Henry Fothergill Chorley, Henry Gay Hewlett

Henry Fothergill Chorley

Autobiography, Memoir, and Letters. Vol. 1

Henry Fothergill Chorley, Henry Gay Hewlett

Henry Fothergill Chorley
Autobiography, Memoir, and Letters. Vol. 1

ISBN/EAN: 9783744689533

Printed in Europe, USA, Canada, Australia, Japan

Cover: Foto ©Raphael Reischuk / pixelio.de

More available books at **www.hansebooks.com**

HENRY FOTHERGILL CHORLEY:

Autobiography, Memoir, and Letters.

COMPILED BY

HENRY G. HEWLETT.

IN TWO VOLUMES.

VOL. I.

LONDON:

RICHARD BENTLEY AND SON,

Publishers in Ordinary to Her Majesty.

1873.

LONDON:
PRINTED BY WILLIAM CLOWES AND SONS,
STAMFORD STREET AND CHARING CROSS.

PREFACE.

A FEW words are necessary to explain my own share in these volumes. In June, 1870, when impressed by the solemn and painful emotions evoked by the death of his most attached friend, Charles Dickens, Chorley requested me, as one of the few younger men who felt an interest in his writings, to undertake the office of his literary executor. A desire to the same effect having been expressed to the gentleman who succeeded to his property, was duly complied with after his death. I found that the autobiography on which my friend had been employed up to that time, and an arrangement for the publication of which had been made with Messrs. Bentley, was left in too incomplete a state to be published as it stood; but that his journals and correspondence afforded ample materials for compiling a memoir wherein its fragments might be embodied, and to which an estimate of his literary career, that could not have been made by himself, would form a fitting supplement. This plan meeting with the approval of his legal representative, effect has been given to it in the present shape. A certain discretion has been exercised by that gentleman in withholding the publication of a few passages of the autobiography, containing strong expressions of opinion or feeling that ought not to be put forth except by a writer still living to justify them. For the most part, however, the statements and opinions of the autobiographer appear without modification.

My task of selection from his correspondence has been materially lightened, by the fact that he had himself assorted it some years before his death, destroying many letters of too private a nature for preservation, and returning others to the friends of the deceased writers. Even with these reductions, the number preserved was considerable; but only specimens have here been given of such characteristic letters as he has retained from the most distinguished of his contemporaries. From those of his correspondents who have survived him, no private communication has been published without authority. In extracting from his elaborate journals, a discretion, such as I believe he would himself have exercised, has been generally observed. No passages have been printed likely to give needless pain to living persons. As respects the dead, I have acted in accordance with his conviction, which is equally my own, that the principle implied in the popular adage, "De mortuis," &c., is liable to be so abused as to render the writing of history impracticable; and that, while it forms no part of a biographer's duty to chronicle trivial infirmities and revive forgotten scandals, he is bound to deal faithfully with all records of act or incident which afford illustrations of character.

The compilation of this memoir, in accordance with the plan thus laid down, has been undertaken as a sacred obligation; how imperfectly it has been executed no one knows better than myself.

My cordial acknowledgments are due to many of Chorley's friends and acquaintance for the assistance they have kindly rendered me; especially to Mrs. Richard Rathbone, for the collection of his letters to herself, and to Sir C. W. Dilke, for the editorial correspondence of the 'Athenæum' placed at my disposal; to Mrs. Procter, Miss Dickens, Mr. Gnosspelius, and Mr. Grüneisen, for their stores of reminiscence; and to Mr. Browning, Mr. Carlyle, and Mr. Procter, for permission to print their letters.

H. G. H.

LONDON, *April,* 1873.

CONTENTS.

c

CHAPTER IV.

CHAPTER V.

CHAPTER VI.

Progress and experiences as a musical critic between
1834 and 1841—Original gifts and acquirements—
Persistence of principle—Conservatism in theory—
Development of taste—Illustrative extracts from
journals—Visits to France in 1836, 1837, and 1839

HENRY FOTHERGILL CHORLEY:

Autobiography, Memoir, and Letters.

CHAPTER I.

Introduction—Early Life and Training in Lancashire—Autobiography.

THE claim of the press to rank as a " Fourth Estate " is now so generally acknowledged, that no apology seems necessary for recording the career of a journalist, however uneventful. Apart from such interest as may attach to the individual, the life of a professional critic, whether of politics, literature, or art, possesses the interest that belongs to the history of his time, to the making of which he materially contributes, by the influence he exerts upon the standards of public opinion and taste. The subject of the present memoir, however,

B

deserves to be remembered for his own sake; as a man who, without advantages of fortune and in spite of many drawbacks, created and maintained for himself an honourable position of independence, even of authority —who, notwithstanding certain infirmities of disposition, exhibited from the outset, and retained to the close of his career, a sincerity of conviction, a rectitude of conduct, a tenderness of heart, that ennobled his calling in the estimation of the world, and endeared his character to those who were admitted to his private friendship.

To some extent the task of Chorley's biographer must be one of vindication. While it would be impossible to claim for him the credit of having enriched our literature with any works of the highest artistic value, there can be no hazard in asserting that his efforts, in more than one province of art and culture, are worthier of a wider recognition than they have yet secured, and that in the field to which he specially devoted himself he was excelled by none of his fellow-labourers. The verdict of one generation is not unfrequently reversed by the next, and peculiarities imperfectly appreciated in a man's lifetime may enhance his posthumous reputation. In Chorley's case, a certain quaintness of manner, half-humorous, half-fastidious, which was reflected in his books, and partly accounted for their failure in obtaining general acceptance, was foremost among the qualities that made them relished by his friends, and added not a little to the attraction of his society. Few men have possessed more of what the greatest poetess of our time—who was one of those friends—has so happily called " the genius to be loved." The circle of his intimates included some of the most distinguished of contemporary men and women; and, in several instances, he has preserved records of the intimacy, which give this memoir a more than personal interest. Had he lived a few months longer, he would have been his own biographer. A considerable portion of these volumes will consist of selections from an unfinished autobiography and a series of journals which were found among his MSS. The arrangement of these extracts, and the insertion in fit order of such letters as he has retained from the most eminent of his deceased correspondents, will form the chief part of my duty. Whenever it is possible, he shall be allowed to speak for himself. For the rest, I shall endeavour to illustrate his career, both as author and critic, by giving some account of his best works, and generally to delineate the man as I knew and esteemed him.

With respect to his family history and the general tenor of his early life and training, the autobiography above mentioned is tolerably complete. As he has written from memory, without revising his childish impressions by subsequent inquiries, his statements of fact and estimates of character are, in the judgment of some members of his family who have seen these pages, occasionally open to correction. I proceed, however, without further preface, to set out such extracts from the manuscript as present a consecutive narrative, not so meagre as to omit any features upon which the autobiographer himself laid stress, nor so diffuse as to exceed the proportions of the posthumous record with which it is now incorporated.

'I am the third son and fourth child of ' John and Jane Chorley, and was born on the ' 15th of December, 1808, at Blackley Hurst, a ' house belonging to the Catholic family of the ' Gerards, near Billinge in Lancashire. My ' father and mother were nominally members ' of the Society of Friends, though neither the ' one nor the other ever wore the dress of that ' religious body, nor conformed to its ascetic ' discipline and testimonies. They were, both ' of them, superior and singular persons; and, ' though differing widely in disposition and ' temperament, maintained an unusual amount ' of affection for each other during their mar- ' ried life, terminated, after sixteen years, by ' the sudden death of my father, on the 15th of ' April, 1816.

'The Chorleys are an old family belonging to
' the gentry of Lancashire, in old times one
' of credit and substance. Two of its members,
' however, were beheaded at Preston, in Lanca-
' shire, in chastisement for their having gone
' out with the Stuarts in 1715,* and their landed
' property was then confiscated. Since that
' time, the principal branch of the family, to
' which I belong, and of which I am the last
' but one, and youngest male survivor, has been
· gradually decaying. My forefathers—at least
' my grandfather, Alexander Chorley, who was
' an ironmaster at Stanley-Bank, near Ashton-
' in-Mackerfield, in Lancashire—had not the
' gift of keeping or of making money. They
' were people of great mother-wit, racy hu-
' mour, and generous dispositions, but san-

* The Chorley family possessed considerable landed estates
in Lancashire; and, according to the county historian, were
seated at Chorley " at or soon after the time of the Conquest."
During the 16th, 17th, and early part of the 18th centuries,
they were sturdy Catholic Recusants, and endured severe
mulcts and penalties for their tenacious adherence to their
faith. (Special Commissions of the Exchequer.—Pub. Rec.
Office.) According to the authority cited by Baines (Hist.
Lancashire, vol. iii. p. 414), Richard Chorley, Esq., the then

' guine and self-willed.   My grandmother
' Chorley was a Fothergill, belonging to an-
' other north-country family of some mark,
' which yielded a popular physician to London
' and a redoubtable preacher to the Society of
' Friends.   She was a woman of strong, severe
' sense.   She brought her husband four sons,
' of whom my father was the eldest, and nine
' daughters.   The sons all perished in the
' very prime of life.   My father dropped down
' dead in his counting-house.   My uncle
' Henry was drowned when on a voyage
' down the Rio del Plata, having fallen over-
' board when he was asleep.   My uncle,
' James Fothergill, died young, of a wasted
' constitution ;   my uncle Charles, of yellow
' fever, in New Orleans.   The daughters were
' longer lived.   All are now gone.

' There was something in the training of

---

head of the family, was alone hanged at Preston for his
complicity in the rebellion of 1715—his son, Charles, who
was also found guilty, dying in prison. The family estates at
Chorley and Walton-cum-Fazakerly were sold by the Com-
missioners of Forfeited Estates to Abraham Crompton, a
Derby banker, for £5550.—(H. G. H.)

' these children sufficiently out of the common
' routine to be worth dwelling on. Born, all
' of them, as I have said, in membership of the
' Society of Friends, and their mother a rigid
' woman, they were still educated—or rather
' educated themselves—with no severity, with
' no outward conformity to the dress and
' statutes of that strange body of religionists.
' My grandfather would not, my grandmother
' could not, control them ; for a more original,
' self-willed family, I believe, was never born
' on the earth, nor one more genially endowed
' with those tastes and fancies which abide no
' restraint nor abnegation of indulgence.
' What is called " the artist temperament "
' belonged to many of them.   They wrote
' verses far above the average of amateur
' verse ; they read something of French and
' Italian.   Two or three of them had aptitude
' for drawing ; and almost all of them a love
' for out-of-the-way reading, and a raciness of
' expression and repartee to which I have
' since met nothing similar.

    ' My aunt Rebecca, the eldest but one, had

' more power to entertain others by her quaint
' sayings and her thoroughly peculiar fancies
' than most women I have known. She re-
' tained it through changes, losses, and deaths,
' and, till the last, kept the same brightness
' of spirit and warmth of heart which made
' her so fascinating as a girl, in spite of a sus-
' picious and hot temper. When scarcely
' fifteen, chancing to stumble on a matrimonial
' advertisement in a newspaper, she answered
' it, so skilfully assuming the character of an
' older woman ready to treat, that a reply came
' directly. Her anonymous correspondent
' seemed to be in earnest, and a gentleman,
' and wrote with such interest that she wrote
' again, still keeping up the masquerade. The
' correspondence went on, the gentleman wax-
' ing warmer and warmer, till he pressed his
' *incognita* for her name and address, declaring
' that he would come from the furthest corner
' of England, merely to make the acquaint-
' ance of the woman who could write with
' such spirit and sweetness, without binding
' her in any way. Then the girl became ter-

' rified, and wrote no more. It was a whim-
' sical trait in her character, that for years
' and years, long after she was a woman
' grown, my aunt, whose handwriting was
' peculiar, would never sign her name at a
' watering-place or in any public book, lest
' she should be identified.

   ' She was staying, as a girl, many years ago,
' in a country-house far removed from towns
' and markets, when one day the family was
' startled by the announced visit of a very
' large party from a distance, who counted on
' finding a dinner. The larder of the house,
' though a hospitable one, happened, by un-
' lucky chance, to be that day well nigh as
' bare as that of Wolf's Crag on the day of
' *Sir William Ashton's* visit, so well provided
' for by *Caleb Balderstone*. The hostess went
' hither and thither in despair. Somehow or
' other the material of the entertainment was got
' together, or represented, one thing only want-
' ing—the dessert. Nothing was to be found
' save a basket of hard, green pears, set aside
' for baking. For better for worse, however,

' by the whimsical girl's counsel, they were
' presented. When she saw them coming, she
' cleared her throat, and in an audible voice
' said to her hostess, at the head of the table,
' " Are not those the famous Cleopatra pears ?"
' She used drily to add, in later years, when,
' mocking at herself, she told this anecdote,
' " My dears, after that no one thought of
" ' refusing them. The dish was cleared."

' " Cleopatra pears " became a by-word in
' our family. They are not a bad symbol of
' much that can be made to pass muster—nay,
' and become popular.

' This family of my grandfather's, too, were
' remarkable for a love of the marvellous ;
' —strange among persons generally more
' vigorous than tender in their composition ;—
' strange, at least in their day, when nervous
' excitement had not taken the lamentable form
' of superstition which we have lately lived
' to see it assume. They noted omens ; they
' dreamt dreams ; they saw ghosts. They had
' their own stories, and warnings, and instances,
' and those who doubted and cross-questioned

' found it better not to do so a second time,
' since the Chorleys were not a patient or
' humble-minded folk, troubled with self-mis-
' trust. In their day, people with narrow
' means (and my grandfather was a poor and
' embarrassed man) stayed much at home;
' and the amount of liberal culture which these
' girls, under Quaker rules, and under the
' more iron grasp of narrow fortunes, contrived
' to get for themselves, in a remote village,
' was something remarkable. There can
' hardly be such households again, now that
' intercourse is so easy, now that books are so
' cheap.

' My mother's maiden name was Jane Wil-
' kinson. She was the child of a second mar-
' riage, born after the death of her father.
' On her mother's side, she belonged to an old
' Cumberland family of the name of Brown-
' sword. These Brownswords, again, were not
' common-place people, though as far asunder
' from my father's family as north is from
' south. My mother's mother was a woman
' of high spirits and indomitable courage—a

' strange mixture of thrift and generosity,
' of cheerful self-sacrifice and overweening
' tyranny. She had been called on when a
' mere girl to decide and to endure; since, at
' the age of eighteen, she was sent by her
' parents on horseback, behind an old servant,
' to arrange and superintend the funeral of a
' brother who had died at a distance from
' home. She was a devoted sick nurse, and
' successively watched the deathbeds of her
' parents, who departed at a patriarchal age,
' of her first husband, Thomas Rutter, a mer-
' chant of Liverpool, by whom she had a son,
' and of a favourite sister; and in this capacity,
' was gentle, untiring, and intrepid; but in
' smooth water, she was too active, too desirous
' of domineering, too resolute to economise
' where no economy was necessary, too full of
' strong will, as well as of strong wit, to be
' judicious as a mother or indulgent as the
' head of a family. " *Give not the staff out of*
' " *thy hand!*" was a phrase often in her
' mouth, after her faculties had failed her.
' Obeyed she would be, and was; for in the

‘ world to which she belonged, the love of
‘ child to parent was expected to come as a
‘ matter of certainty and of duty.

‘ My mother, at least, was an affectionate
‘ and a dutiful, if not an obedient, daughter.
‘ She had the timid, tremulous organisation
‘ said to belong to an old man’s child; and
‘ being full of tastes and capacities for enjoy-
‘ ment, with which her more robust parent had
‘ no sympathy, and more alive to the pain of
‘ rebuke than any one I have known, managed
‘ to creep betwixt the meshes of the net of
‘ household discipline, to peep at what stood
‘ with her for the world, and to indulge her
‘ fancies for poetry, romance, and art (as art
‘ was understood in those primitive, narrow
‘ days). Had she fallen into a more genial
‘ soil, she might have won distinction as an
‘ authoress; since, when a mere child, living
  in a quiet market-town in Cumberland, she
‘ showed not so much the desire to scribble
‘ as the power to imitate, which precedes, in
‘ ninety-nine cases out of a hundred, the power
‘ to create. I have before me the manuscript

‘ of a novel, the formal childish writing beau-
‘ tiful, the age of its writer considered, and
‘ perfect as to spelling, by which it is evident
‘ that the small person had got hold of
‘ “ Evelina ” — had caught the tone of the
‘ characters and the time of the dialogue. To
‘ the very last years of her life she could amuse
‘ herself and relieve her mind by writing
‘ verses; and in the rhymes of the old woman,
‘ as well as of the girl, there is a vein of true
‘ poetry, of real fancy, and of real feeling. She
‘ was very lovely on a small scale, with shy
‘ eyes, a fresh complexion, and a perfectly-
‘ formed mouth, and hair of that sunny colour
‘ which womanhood ripens into auburn.
‘ While she was a girl, her widowed mother,
‘ who had been for some time resident at
‘ her native place, Wigton, in Cumberland,
‘ brought her to live in Liverpool; being
‘ induced to change her residence by the
‘ settlement there of my mother’s half-brother,
‘ John Rutter, who, for nearly half a century,
‘ honourably practised physic in that place.

‘ Of him, too, I must say a word, at the

‘ risk of being over elaborate in matters of
‘ pedigree and family-picture, because he, too,
‘ was a character, in some respects rare at
‘ any time, but singularly rare, considering the
‘ circumstances and opportunities of his posi-
‘ tion.   God never created a more noble-
‘ hearted, generous man than he was ; few men
‘ have ever been more zealous in their calling,
‘ less pedantic in the task of perpetual self-edu-
‘ cation and qualification. A dread of the shame
‘ of debt, an excellent liberality in the exercise
‘ of his profession, the curious mixture of
‘ personal modesty and sagacious decision in
‘ his medical practice, possibly, too, his hand-
‘ some person, established him in· his birth-
‘ place, after years of probation, as first
‘ physician ; but his ways were as little like
‘ the world’s ordinary ways as those of the
‘ rest of the persons among whom we four
‘ Chorley children were brought up. He had
‘ remarkable stores of knowledge, which to
‘ the last he increased, yet he could not en-
‘ dure intellectual society, the collision and
‘ discussion of opinions. Born and remaining

' till his decease a member of the Society of
' Friends,. he had nothing in common with
' their habits or requirements, read what he
' pleased, dressed as he pleased, for relaxation
' became a keen whist player (which suited
' his taciturn habits). A good deal courted, I
' have reason to think, by women when he was
' young, no man was less throughout his life
' a courtier of women—perhaps, because being
' honourable beyond his kind he never felt
' justified in thinking of marriage till he had
' reached the age at which romance (on either
' side) ceases, and convenience begins. At
' that point, family affection brought a charge
' upon him (it would be ungrateful to say,
' cast a burden into his lap), which he accepted
' wholly, nobly, devotedly; and the acceptance
' of which so occupied him as to leave him
' with small time or fancy for more selfish
' interests. At my father's death he came
' forward to stand betwixt his half-sister, with
' her four children, and penury; and thence-
' forward his life seemed to find its duties
' and, in some degree, I am glad to think,

' its rewards also, in the family whom he
' had adopted.   .

  ' Over all these original, imperfectly-edu-
' cated persons, the ordinances and the usages
' of the Society of Friends hung like a pall of
' conformity, heavy enough to inspire them
' with certain characteristics, but so oppressive
' as to make escape and insincerity inevitable.
' It would be difficult to conceive a worse edu-
' cation for mind and heart. On the one side,
' a narrow, ascetic, mystical sectarianism, in-
' cluding the minute formalities of discipline,
' but not including the rallying-points of an
' established creed; on the other, worldly pur-
' suits and pleasures, partaken of by snatches,
' without those safeguards which good breed-
' ing and good manners substitute for higher
' moral principle and precept among people of
' the world. I have always rated those from
' whom I have sprung on both sides, in no
' respect more highly than in this, that people
' of their quick spirits and vigorous intellect
' were so little affected by such training.

  ' Then, with persons of lively humour, the

' forms of worship in use among the Society
' of Friends, the curious manifestations of
' scruple among the narrow, and the adroit
' relaxations of discipline among the more
' genial, were not calculated to engender that
' spirit of reverence without which there is
' no religious training for the young. There
' was a feature in the preaching among the
' Society of Friends especially calculated to
' annoy persons of quick temperament and
' rebellious understandings, namely, the per-
' sonality which at times could be thrown into
' it. Not only in the domestic visits, which
' the accepted ministers of the society are in
' the habit of paying to all families in member-
' ship, but on such painful occasions as funerals
' (which are attended by female as well as
' male relatives of the deceased) have I heard
' those known to be liberal or suspected
' of disaffection marked out for reproof and
' counsel, with a directness of application
' which admitted of no mistake on the part of
' any hearer. The last time that I ever
' entered a Friends' meeting-house was to.

' attend the funeral of my good and honoured
' uncle, which was largely attended by many
' of his townsfolk, who loved his memory.
' I was one of a group of survivors thus
' lectured by a loud, harsh, ignorant man,
' who, on account of our having quitted the
' Society, would not lose so timely a chance
' of administering a severe and warning casti-
' gation. It was impossible to feel either re-
' sentment or shame. The insults of fanatical
' self-importance have no power over those
' against whom they are launched, except
' they fall on persons of bad conscience or
' credulous habits of mind; but there is
' many a one and many another whom such
' training on the one hand, and such arro-
' gance on the other, have driven loose from
' all their early moorings, and have flung
' into that shifting sea of contempt for all
' religious profession and disbelief in all creeds
' which it is most perilous for the young to
' traverse.

' This was not the case, happily, with either
' my father or my mother; yet they did not

' pass through such a discipline of education,
' which is no education, without bad results to
' themselves and to their children. We saw
' from infancy the statutes of the Society to
' which we nominally belonged evaded; for
' my mother painted flowers and practised
' music. We conceived an intense and weary
' distaste for the manner of worship, in
' which the general alternatives were tiresome
' silence or the maunderings of some uncouth
' and illiterate person; and yet we heard the
' world and the world's usages criticised as
' sharply as if they were not in an awkward
' way approached and imitated by our parents.

' It was yet another disadvantage, in one
' respect, that we were born and brought up
' in the country without companionship with
' other children. On my father's marriage
' with my mother, they set up house in a
' small cottage not far from Warrington,
' which had been originally, I suspect, a
' barn, subsequently divided into closets
' rather than rooms, to serve as shooting-
' box for its owner, or pleasure-house for

' some one among his *sultanas*. This owner,
' Colonel ——, belonging to a family who
' had considerable landed property in Lanca-
' shire and Cheshire, was one of those wild
' provincial imitations of the town *Mohocks*—
' the Camelfords and Delavals—the race of
' which is, I hope, extinct, though they have
' left behind them traces and traditions, of
' which persons brought up in towns have
' little idea. From among such people and
' such traditions did the Brontë sisters gather
' the materials for their novels—books which
' will have a value for the future historian
' of English society, if even they cease to
' be read for the rude power and romance
' put forth in them. Colonel —— was a
' brutal, licentious man, full of life and spirits
' for every quality of mischief, who made
' the corner of Lancashire in which he lived
' ring with tales of his debauchery and of his
' practical jokes. He it was who invited a
' starved company of mountebanks to dine
' with the clergyman at Newton-in-the-
' Willows on Sunday, and stationed himself

' in the post-office opposite, to see the dis-
' comfiture of the poor creatures as they
' came out, when the hoax should be dis-
' covered. But the heartless jester sat there
' in vain. The clergyman was a kind man,
' and on comparing notes with player-king,
' player-queen, pantaloon, clown, and the rest,
' as they gradually assembled, discovered
' how all had been tricked. "Well," said
' he, "ladies and gentlemen, I must not lose
' the pleasure of your company, though I
' had not the pleasure of inviting you;" and
' he detained them to dinner and (the story
' goes on to say) fed them well, leaving to
' their tormentor the pleasure of sitting and
' waiting. But it was not every one who had
' courage or power, like this cordial parson,
' thus to thwart the will and pleasure of
' Colonel ——, so that his name became a
' terror in the district. His death, caused by
' apoplexy—mistaken for a drunken fit by his
' pot-companions—was sudden and awful; and
' after his death were circulated the usual
' stories; such as, that he really was not dead,

'but had allowed a figure to be buried, by
'way of escape from his creditors; that "he
'"walked," and the like. It is certain that the
'guests of my father and mother who visited
'them at Deane Cottage believed themselves
'to have been disturbed there by some unac-
'countable noises, others by apparitions; and
'the bad reputation which Colonel —— left
'behind him in some sort communicated itself
'to every residence belonging to him. Gol-
'borne Park was also reputed to be the scene
'of supernatural visitations; and in that
'house, too, the members of my father's
'family conceived themselves to have wit-
'nessed unearthly appearances. But those
'who are apt to note ghostly wonders, will
'find them everywhere; and, as experience
'has made me familiar with the active im-
'aginations of the race to which I belong,
'I cannot believe that any of the tales which
'I heard from an early age, told and re-told
'with a minuteness of circumstance, which
'increased in precision and polish as time
'went on, are more to be relied on than the

' majority of their fascinating family. I recur
' to them, not as incidents which I can warrant
' as having happened, but merely because
' their influence gave a breath and a tincture
' to the atmosphere in which we were born
' and brought up. I cannot recollect that we
' ever experienced any practical or active suf-
' fering from the fear of ghosts, as children ;
' but I, for one, certainly believed ·'in their
' existence as a child, in imitation of, and
' reliance on, the elder people who were above
' and about me.

  ' My mother was married the day when she
' came of age—more unformed in character, I
' imagine, than most girls who have reached the
' age of twenty-one and entered married life.
' With her, this want of form merely implied
' want of courage, not want of affection, not
' want of gifts, many and various, not want
' of desire to do what was right. Courage
' my father was not able to give her. Perhaps
' they did not live long enough together for
' him to perceive its absence ; perhaps the
' gentleness may have been a characteristic

' which would have endeared her to him had
' he thought upon it. But, indeed, so far as I
' can learn or recollect, he had been as little
' trained as she was; and both he and she
' were subject to such influences of a sec-
' tarian position as would defy or neutralise
' any training whatsoever, supposing the chil-
' dren subjected to them were by nature
' endowed with genius. I suspect that they
' loved each other dearly, and thought little
' of the future—nothing that the four chil-
' dren whom they brought into the world
' were to come after them, and however like
' them, MUST be "other, *though* the same."
' And they married, as I have said, to live
' in a retired part of Lancashire, and early
' to make acquaintance with difficulties of
' fortune. My mother inherited some money
' from her north-country ancestors, but wil-
' lingly and trustingly (without compulsion or
' question) allowed a portion of this to be ab-
' sorbed in my father's business, which was that
' of an iron-worker, at Ashton-in-Mackerfield,
' and which, from the time of his marriage,

' became less and less profitable. Her married
' life was a happy one, but it was largely so
' because she never inquired nor looked for-
' ward. She had her materials for enjoyment
' within herself and in the love of those close
' to her. She inherited from the North her
' simple tastes and economical habits, and
' probably had less of show, and luxury, and
' enjoyment out of the money which came to
' her by inheritance, and lived to see it to do
' less good, than most women, young, beau-
' tiful, and gifted, who have ever inherited
' money.

' My sister was born at Deane Cottage; my
' eldest brother at Penswick House—a house of
' little more pretension, which stood by the
' side of a by-road, and belonged to a family of
' Catholics. My brother John and, lastly, my-
' self were born at Blackley Hurst.* This
' was a dilapidated country-seat, near Billinge,
' in Lancashire, one of those which belonged

* " *Wigan parish—Billinge township.* Blake Hurst, now
called Blackley Hurst, existing in the sixteenth century. . . .
the property of Sir Robert Gerard, Bart."—Baine's Hist.
Lancashire, new ed. vol. ii. p. 190. (H. G. H.)

' to the Catholic family of the Gerards, and
' which was let to my father at a reduced
' rent. The country thereabouts, in those days
' thinly sprinkled with inhabitants, is open and
' varied, affording some wide prospects, and
' diversified by a range of hills, some of which
' are crowned with beacons so marked in form
' as to make on a child's mind that impression
' at once real, but visionary, which never
' afterwards fades out of it. It is upwards of
' half a century since I have set eyes on any
' corner of that district, which I left when
' little more than an infant. Yet it has grown
' into my heart, and rises before me as I
' write, as a pleasant, breezy landscape or
' landscapes.

' If my own recollections go back to a very
' early date in life, it is probably because my
' powers of observation were prematurely
' sharpened by being either left to myself or
' living with grown people. As boys from
' childhood, my two brothers " cronied " to-
' gether, leaving the youngest, weakest, and
' ugliest as the odd one ; and my sister early

' became my mother's companion. I have
' thus, from infancy, been alone as regards
' family confidence or comradeship ; and the
' subsequent periods of life at which this
' condition of solitude has been partly coun-
' teracted have been few and far between.
' My father was fond of me, however, as of
' a sort of *Benjamin,* since he used to take
' me on his knee while he quoted that line
' from Chaucer—

 ' " And spare my Gamelyn, because he's young."

' I think, too, he must have discerned some-
' thing of the adventurer in my composition ;
' for I recollect his saying, when I was a small
' child, that " if I were turned loose in the
' " streets of London, he should have no fear
' " of my losing my way.' "
 ' We were all quaint children : I suppose,
' from our circumstances of fortune and posi-
' tion. We invented names, and plays, and
' novels (my sister was a famous inventor, and
' much in request), and made a children's life
' in that old house, with its neglected shrub-

' beries, far different from the lives of children
' who go to school or have playfellows, or
' belong to people who *are* rich and who are
' *not* original.

' We had names and nomenclatures of our
' own; the filaments that straggled from the
' twigs of an old honeysuckle, that, with aid
' of a tall white rose-tree, clambered half-way
' up a larch at the spot where a path down to
' the garden turned off from the grass-plot in
' front of the house, were " Hercules' back,"
' and so on. I cannot recollect either learning
' to read or to write; but a letter exists written
' by me before I was three years and a half
' old; and before that time, I had heard and
' caught up verses, since I distinctly recollect
' weeping at an elegy called " The Nun " (by
' whom I do not remember), which began—

    ' " With each perfection dawning in her mind,
      ' " All Beauty's treasure opening on her cheek,"

' and at a verse in " Jemmy Dawson "—

    ' " O then, her mourning-coach was called,
      ' " The sledge moved slowly on before;
    ' " Though borne in a triumphal car,
      ' " She had not loved her favourite more!"

' I have since never endured the sorrow of
' parting and bereavement (and few of my age
' have endured that sorrow much oftener)
' without this stanza rising up to my mind un-
' bidden. Such infant impressions made on
' fancy and feeling are indelible I have no
' remembrance of reading any child's book
' till at a much later period, nor of having
' been set to read at any task. Some teaching
' there was, but it could not have been heavy
' or steadily enforced; but dreams, and no-
' tions, and humours had already grown into
' my mind untaught, never to be dislodged
' thence.

' When I was somewhere about four years
' old, my father removed from Blackley Hurst
' to Smithy Brook, a square, ugly, new house
' by the side of the road betwixt Warrington
' and Wigan, near the latter town, with a
' square, ugly, new garden. Matters were
' going ill with the lock-making business; and
' the forlorn country-seat where I was born
' was tumbling down with damp and dry-rot;
' but for us children the change was a change

‘ for the worse. The high-road was mean and
‘ beaten—in no respect rural. We had squalid
‘ cottages close to us; and from a more remote
‘ cluster of these, called Goose Green, came
‘ that child’s first sorrow which is called a
‘ schoolmaster, by whom our reading, writing,
‘ and ciphering were to be perfected. He
‘ was an inefficient, civil old creature—who
‘ spoke broad Lancashire, at which we mocked
‘ —in no respect qualified to inspire any one
‘ with a love for learning, or a fear of him-
‘ self. I think he must have taught me the
‘ rudiments of arithmetic, since I distinctly
‘ recollect the loathing I conceived of slate
‘ and pencil, and sitting over my sum with a
‘ mind wandering heaven knows where—be-
‘ yond the reach or range, at all events, of
‘ any work which was to be done. But de-
‘ lights were to be got out of the slate; it
‘ was an amusement to try to draw on it;
‘ and my early drawings took no more pic-
‘ turesque forms than recurring borders and
‘ arabesques, which were dignified by the
‘ name of “ beltages,” and in which the fancy

' for decoration (if I may not call it a love of
' art) manifested itself distinctly.

'Among the other childish recollections of
' that time, were preparations to be made
' against a gang of housebreakers, headed by a
' notorious man of the name of George Lyon,
' and the experiences of death in the decease
' of a neighbour's son by scarlet fever, and
' of an aged woman, Mrs. Bradshaw, who had
' lived on the opposite side of the lane to our
' house, and who had been good-natured to
' us when children. The last is printed into
' my mind, by recollecting how my mother
' was called in to mediate among the sur-
' vivors, who were at daggers drawn, which
' should inherit "*the* silk gown," the most
' precious amongst the effects of the deceased,
' who was, yet, no pauper. Then there were
' such graver events (little graver, however,
' to a child) as the escape from Elba of Buo-
' naparte—and, in those days, nine out of ten
' Dissenting men and women were Buona-
' partists—and the excitement produced in
' harassed, war-worn England by the intelli-

' gence. It is a mistake to fancy that children
' take no part in such things, or that they do
' so as merely apeing the serious business of
' their elders. Country children, at least,
' are, or were, stirred by public events without
' fully understanding their entire import and
' bearing; and I do not remember the day of
' my life at which I did not earnestly believe
' that I was a Liberal, and feel that indigna-
' tion against "the powers that be" which
' time has made less violent.

' It was while we were living at Smithy
' Brook, that I recollect first hearing music,
' and hearing it with that passion which, if it
' had been understood and provided for, might
' possibly have conducted me to some emi-
' nence in the art. My mother, as I have
' said, who possessed a good deal of the artist
' temperament, had struggled to learn to play
' on the pianoforte after she was a married
' woman, of course with small success; for
' her fingers were stiff, and her lessons had
' been few, and her master, a country organist,
' was a bad one. Her only care, moreover, was

' to pick out Scotch, or Irish, or Welsh melo-
' dies, or the few songs which she had heard ·
' as fashionable during her honeymoon visit
' to London in 1800. So far as I can recol-
' lect, her three music-books contained two
' single morsels by composers of credit,
' Haydn's " Mermaid's Song " and an arrange-
' ment of Handel's " Water Music." The
' first she used to sing somehow with a sweet
' but undeveloped voice; the latter was beyond
' her reach. And I hardly know why I should
' have delighted to open the book at that
' page if it had not been that the name
' " Water Music " may have suggested some-
' thing rich and pompous. I cannot explain
' when or where I began to associate the
' printed symbols with the possible sounds of
' music. But long ere I could put my hand
' on a pianoforte, I could read the notes some-
' how, and somehow represent to myself that
' which they signified.

' We removed, early in the year 1816, from
' Smithy Brook to Green End, about three
' miles from St. Helens, in Lancashire. This

‘ had been a small, old-fashioned house, to
‘ which a new portion, or wing, had been
‘ added, the whole making a pleasant, irregular
‘ residence. The garden was full of cherry-
‘ trees, and one had been trained over the
‘ window of the nursery or school-room. The
‘ sweep before the house was very rich in
‘ flowering shrubs of the commoner kinds—
‘ double-blossomed cherries, lilacs, locust-trees,
‘ laburnums, guelder-roses, syringas ; and the
‘ gate, which looked towards Billinge Hill,
‘ and from which the house where I was born
‘ was distinctly visible, was overshadowed by
‘ a fine lime-tree, which, in summer, was full of
‘ fragrance, and, as Coleridge says, “ musical
‘ with bees.” The enjoyment of that peaceful
‘ view, and of those country things was felt at
‘ the time, and lives in my mind freshly now ;
‘ and the sight of one of the well-known shrubs
‘ in St. James’s Park, or, even more, the scent,
‘ has again and again taken me off to those old
‘ days, like a spell, when I have been bustling
‘ towards Temple Bar, with my head full of
‘ pain, my heart of care, and my pocket of

' proofs. Even now, while I but write about
' the place, I am stopped, by a sort of sadness,
' to ask if such sadness be real, or merely that
' sentimentality which certain persons never
' outgrow. The picture, however, is clear,
' and abounding in shade and blossom at all
' events. And Green End seems to me now
' the happiest place of residence I ever in-
' habited. From it we removed to Liverpool
' in the year 1819-20. I have never seen it
' since, nor since then sojourned in the
' country, save as a rare visitor. But I often
' think that it is town-birds who best relish
' and appreciate country sights, sounds, and
' things; and know that with myself, at least
' —though I should not be believed on oath
' by any friend or acquaintance I have—it
' is a love that " fadeth not away." The
' great and intimate pleasure which land-
' scape painting has always given me, the
' satisfaction I find in the wonderful new
' photographs of bare trees which I have
' lived to see brought to such perfection,
' date back, I believe, to those three years

' betwixt the seventh and tenth of my
' life.

'We had hardly been settled in this
' pleasant place many weeks before the 15th
' of April, 1816, arrived. On that day my
' father, who was used to ride away to his
' lock-making business, took leave of my
' mother as usual, and came home no more,
' since he fell dead from the seat before his
' counting-house desk. Times had been grow-
' ing worse with him for some years, and
' this it may have been which had caused the
' haggard look and the loss of bulk, remarked
' after his death; or they may have been
' signs of the organic heart-disease which took
' him from us. The dismay, terror, and con-
' fusion of those days is like a thing of last
' week; and every minute detail comes back
' to me as I begin to think over the painful
' scene. My mother was like some timid
' creature broken to pieces by the shock of
' an earthquake, unable to do much more
' than weep, and submit, and endure. On
' hearing the news of her husband's sudden

' illness (for thus was the catastrophe broken
' to her), she had set off from Green End, on
' foot, to get to him ; but she was met in the
' road, at the distance of a mile or two from
' the house, by kind friends who were hasten-
' ing to her. Then it was necessary to bring
' relatives together, and my mother's and my
' father's had not much cordiality one for the
' other ; and then there was the day of the
' funeral, and the dinner after the funeral.
' We were within the pale of old country and
' Dissenting customs. It was necessary that a
' dinner should be given after the funeral,
' though it was agreed on both sides of the
' house, that ruin was in it. And, by the
' usages of the sect to which my parents nomi-
' nally belonged, females as well as males
' attended the dead to their last home. My
' father's is in the graveyard of a small meet-
' ing-house belonging to the Society of Friends
' at Penketh, not far from Warrington, at the
' edge of a patch of common-land ; a small,
' still resting-place, in which the separate
' tenements were distinguished only by turfed

' mounds. Time has softened the usages of
' the Society of Friends in this respect. They
' have now tombstones in their graveyards,
' simply inscribed with name, age, and date
' of decease.'

CHAPTER II.

Autobiography—*continued.*

' On my father's death, my mother's half-
' brother, John Rutter, of Liverpool, stood
' betwixt herself and want. There was no
' money on the other side of the house which
' could have availed for our assistance. There
' was no male relative to interpose; and I
' think there was not any extreme tenderness
' for our young and timid mother, than whom
' I have known no being less qualified to cope
' with the practical difficulties of life. We
' remained at Green End betwixt three and
' four years, which seem to me now double
' that length of time; perhaps because they
' were years of wakening—years, too, of some
' suffering; and then, for the first time, I be-

' gan to feel the yearnings for companionship
' which beset one of an affectionate nature, a
' fanciful imagination, and a social humour,
' placed by circumstances in a solitary position.
' On her widowhood, my mother possessed
' herself of my sister as her chosen com-
' panion, and my two elder brothers, as I
' have said, " cronied " together. I was the
' smallest, the worst-looking, the most ner-
' vous ; not a coward, though reported such,
' because of great physical excitability ; to-
' tally inexpert with my hands and at all
' the manly games in which boys delight ;
' therefore mocked at, and left alone, without
' any excessive persecution, but without any
' influence to encourage, assist, or befriend me.

' During a part of our stay at Green End,
' we had private tutors, such as they were.
' One, a man of humble origin, who had
' aspired to ordination in the Church, and
' filled up the interval till he could be ap-
' pointed to a Yorkshire curacy by teaching
' us some Latin. Another, a curiosity in the
' shape of a crack-brained Irish Methodist,

' who used to teach us or not, as pleased him ;
' to fly into rages, and to start away into ec-
' centric readings of books totally beyond our
' years and capacity : a being, in short, as
' utterly unfit to restrain four singular and
' solitary children as any creature that could
' have been fished up from the depths of
' Ireland or the bottoms of Methodism. The
' teaching came to nought; the connection
' could not last; and after a vain trial or two
' more to procure for us something more or-
' derly and customary in the way of private
' education, we three boys were put to a not
' bad day-school at St. Helens, where we were
' " brought on," as the school-phrase is, in
' the classical languages, and in writing and
' arithmetic, and, I think, were well considered
' by the masters.

' But from first to last, to me all schooling
' was intolerable. I was hopelessly idle—
' perhaps because, in some things, I was pre-
' cociously quick, having been started in the
' world with a memory of no common compass
' and strength, and with that sort of *divining*

' nature which is one of the elements of the
' artist temperament. Had this been under-
' stood, and had this been worked towards
' in forming character and in developing such
' talents as God gave me, my life might have
' yielded special results, in place of the uni-
' versal indications which are all it ever will
' yield.   But this was not seen, not appre-
' hended, perhaps could not be; and I had
' then, as now, a physically feeble tempera-
' ment, in which irritability and languor
' were oddly mixed up.   This may have
' saved me from desperate outbreaks to get
' at a life I liked, which I might else have
' ventured. Such resisting power as I had
' was merely sufficient to prevent my learning
' anything that I did not covet to learn, com-
' pletely or correctly. Had I been apprenticed
' to a musician, or to a draftsman, or to an
' architect, I fancy I might have become dis-
' tinguished. As it was, Latin and Greek did
' me small good; and as I had little company
' to my liking (though, let me again remem-
' ber, little unkindness), the one weakest gift

'which belonged to the others—a certain
'fantasy and taste for numbers—must needs
'push itself forward, since no stronger mem-
'ber of its family had room or play; and
'I began, almost as soon as I could begin to
'write, to divert myself, and to excite atten-
'tion among injudicious folk, by scribbling.

'Probably *no* English children of the next
'generation will ever be made to understand
'how intense is the value, and how lasting the
'impression, of the things that speak to the
'mind of a child in my plight, as pleasures
'and revelations. A character in those days,
'whom I regarded with extreme curiosity
'and interest, was an *ex*-Catholic priest. He
'had left the Jesuits' College at Douai, had
'embraced Protestantism, had made his es-
'cape from France during the troubles of
'the first Revolution, and was accustomed to
'recount the breathless perils of his escape,
'in a sort of set narration, which he was
'asked to deliver at the little tea-drinkings
'and gatherings round about. Of this des-
'cribed adventure, which he told in a longer

' or a shorter version, I could now — forty
' years later—repeat portions, so vividly is it
' painted on my recollection.

' Our neighbours at Green End, though
' kindly, were common-place enough : a group
' of families, with habits, ways, and pleasures
' such as those which Mrs. Gaskell has des-
' cribed in her inimitable " Cranford." There
' was the great house, accessible from ours by
' a shady little lane, banked with wood-sorrel,
' up which I think I see my mother walking
' dressed for dinner, bare-headed, under a
' parasol, on a hot summer afternoon. There
' was the parsonage with its clergyman, a
' good, warm-hearted, unselfish creature, as
' kind to us as if we had not been Dissenters
' (to him) of a most unintelligible pattern.
' There was a family of sisters, who had
' among them some beauty, a little music,
' universal skill in needlework, and one who
' had once been to London. And there was a
' touchy lady, looked down upon because her
' origin was supposed not to have been suf-
' ficiently choice. It seems to me, on look-

' ing back, as if all these people were
' reasonably happy, in spite of their little
' humours and ambitions. Vicissitudes, how-
' ever, broke out among them, even before
' we quitted that corner of Lancashire; and
' though Green End was a pleasant home, it
' was no resting-place for a widow with three
' odd boys to educate and start in life.

' Our removal from Green End was decided
' by the violent illness of my Liverpool uncle,
' who well-nigh died of a typhus fever. That
' illness decided the current of my life, though
' little could any one guess it at the time. A
' relation or family connection of his,* Mrs.
' Rathbone, of Green Bank, daughter of
' Richard Reynolds, of Bristol, the munifi-
' cent Quaker philanthropist, insisted, accord-
' ing to her wont, on his being nursed there
' during his convalescence; insisted on my
' mother (who had been summoned from us
' to be his head-nurse) accompanying him;
' and, with delicate and considerate kindness,

---

* Dr. Rutter was the first cousin of this lady's husband,
Mr. William Rathbone. (H. G. H.)

' would have us children all four join *her*
' there at her country-house, within four miles
' of Liverpool. To myself, that visit was the
' spark which falls on tinder. You may put
' it out, but not till it has burnt a hole.

' Hannah Mary Rathbone was a noble and
' fascinating woman; the most faithful of
' wives, the most devoted of mothers, the
' most beneficent of friends. In 1819, when I
' stayed at Green Bank, she was in the last
' ripeness of her maturity, looking older than
' her years, but as beautiful as any picture
' which can be offered by freshest youth.
' Though she was nominally a member of the
' Society of Friends, she never conformed to
' its uniform. Her profuse white hair, which
' had been white from an early age, was cut
' straight like a man's, to lie simply on her
' forehead. Above this was her spotless cap
' of white net, rescued from meagreness by a
' quilled border and a sort of scarf of the same
' material round it—a head-dress as pictu-
' resque, without being queer, as if its wearer
' had studied for years how to arrange it. Her

' gown was always a dark silk, with a quantity
' of delicate muslin to swathe the throat, and
' a shawl which covered the stoop of her short
' figure—the shawl never gay, though mostly
' rich. But the face was simply one of the most
' beautiful faces (without regularity) that I
' have ever seen; beautiful in spite of its
' being slightly underhung; the eyes were so
' deep, brilliant, and tender; the tint was so
' fresh, the expression was so noble and so
' affectionate; and the voice matched the face
' —so low it was, so kind, so cordial, and (to
' come back to my point) as I fancied, so
' irresistibly intimate, which means apprecia-
' ting. The welcome of that elderly woman to
' the awkward, scared, nervous child who en-
' tered her house, is to me one of the recol-
' lections which mark a life, as having decided
' its aims, by encouraging its sympathies.

' She had been throughout her life the ad-
' mired friend and counsellor of many distin-
' guished men, all belonging to the liberal
' school of ideas and philosophies, which were
' wakened, especially in the world of Dissenters,

' by the first French Revolution. One of so
' fearless a brain, and so tenderly religious a
' heart, and so pure a moral sense as she I
' have never known. Her moral courage was
' indomitable; her manners shy, gentle, and
' caressing.

    ' Since that time, I have been in many
' luxurious houses; but anything like the de-
' licious and elegant comfort of Green Bank
' during her reign I have never known—
' plenty without coarseness; exquisiteness with-
' out that super-delicacy which oppresses by its
' extravagance. It was a house to which the
' sick went to be nursed, and the benevolent to
' have their plans carried out. It was any-
' thing but a hide-bound or Puritanical house ;
' for the library was copious, and novels and
' poems were read aloud in the parlours, and
' such men as William Roscoe, Robert Owen,
' Sylvester of Derby, Combe of Edinburgh,
' came and went. There was a capital garden ;
' there was a double verandah—and if I live to
' see all the glories of sun, moon, and seven stars,
' I shall never see that verandah equalled ; and

' there was a pianoforte—not like my mother's
' pianoforte at Green End (which Dickens must
' have known, else he could never have de-
' scribed Miss Tox's instrument, with the
' wreath of sweet peas round its maker's name,
' in " Dombey ")—kept under lock and key.
' There were water and a boat;—but more,
' there was a touch of the true fire from Heaven
' in the owner of all these delights which
' spoke to me in a way hardly to be described,
' never to be forgotten. In the case of some
' people, even from childhood upwards, one
' judges; with others, one hopes; with others,
' one believes; with others, one learns; with
' a few, *one knows;* and those few, as I have
' said, decide one's life.

' How that great, and good, and gentle
' woman ruled her family—having been left
' a widow at middle age—how *toned* them to
' a standard such as few even try to reach,
' many, very many, living know as well as I.
' Few have influenced so many by their affec-
' tions, by their reason, by their understanding,
' so honourably as that retiring, delicate wo-

' man ; and it is a pleasure (not without tears
' in it) to me to think that when we are all no
' more, some one, untouched by family par-
' tiality or tradition, shall say this much by
' way of laying a leaf on a modest, but a very
' holy, grave.

' The manner in which I played and picked
' out tunes on that small square pianoforte at
' Green Bank, and began to read music long
' ere I could name a note, connecting the ideas
' of sound and symbol, strikes me now—who
' have since seen much of the beginnings of
' musicians—as arguing propensity for the art
' above the average. On the other side of
' the lane, close to Green Bank, was another
' house, inhabited by a lady with five daughters.
' One of these was a pianist ; and she had
' Handel's Overtures bound in a book—piano-
' forte arrangements, I think, by Mazzinghi—
' and my quick precocity as to music excited
' her interest. She was then a full-grown
' young lady, while I was only little more than
' a child, but was good-natured enough to send
' for me and to play these to me. Overtures

' to " Acis," " Alcina," " Atalanta "—above all,
' the royal " Occasional Overture " (and royal
' it is, with its prelude, and its fanfares, and its
' march).   Her playing was not good, and the
' greatness of Handel was in no wise repre-
' sented by the arrangement; and yet somehow,
' even from those attempts at transcripts I
' derived a pleasure, an impression of power,
' and a feeling as if something magnificent and
' true had been shown me—the same impres-
' sion which a child, however incapable of rea-
' soning, may derive from Milton's noble ver-
' sification, or from Shakespeare's divine in-
' sights into nature—something ignorant, in-
' complete — irresistible.   By such curious,
' broken steps, I have often thought many of
' the English destined really to cultivate art
' or letters must walk upwards. Do academies
' suit our rude, independent natures, our incom-
' plete sympathies—at least in Art ?   But the
' kindness of this lady did not fall on altogether
' ungrateful soil.   It could not make a musi-
' cian of me, for " the stars " were too inex-
' orably opposed to it ; but it helped to awaken

' in me a desire, which has never wholly died
' out, in my turn to show kindness to those
' having tastes and tendencies without means
' of indulging them.

' It was at Green Bank, too, that I saw
' authors and poets for the first time. Roscoe
' had long been the attached and intimate
' friend of Mrs. Rathbone ; more so than ever,
' as far as her constant good offices could prove
' it, after the failure of the Liverpool Bank,
' in which he had become interested. It was
' the period when Elizabeth Fry's notable
' efforts to amend prison discipline were ex-
' citing men's attention. He was about some
' work on the subject, and used perpetually
' to come and go, with plans and papers,
' and letters and reports, for comparison and
' consultation. It was wonderful to observe
' the eagerness with which those two enthu-
' siastic people went heart, soul, temper, and
' passion into the matter, under the certainty
' of large and generous results.

' Campbell, too, was down at Liverpool that
' winter, giving his lectures on poetry at the

' Royal Institution. I heard much of him,
' and I could then have repeated by heart the
' best part of " O'Connor's Child ;" but I never
' then saw him. I heard, too, of other Scottish
' celebrities — a good deal of the Dugald
' Stewarts, with whom Mrs. Rathbone had in-
' tercourse. It was another air I was breathing
' to any that I had ever breathed before. After
' having breathed it, I was never again the
' same creature that I had been. To those who
' enjoy the advantages now so largely mul-
' tiplied and so widely diffused, the remem-
' brance of " these inklings of education " may
' seem puerile, perhaps caricatured; but as I
' belong to the class of those for whom in-
' tercourse and occupation have always done
' more than lonely study, in whom production
' has quickened thought, rather than thought
' suggested production—at once desultory and
' determined, indolent and feverishly active—
' it may be still curious to some of like tem-
' perament, under better dispensations, to be
' told how were certain veins opened and cer-
' tain pursuits set a-going.

' We removed to Liverpool in the year 1819,
' and we three boys were placed at the school
' of the Royal Institution, then headed by the
' Rev. John Monk, an urbane, good-natured
' man, and a fair scholar; but where little,
' virtually, was taught save Latin and Greek—
' an odd training for boys among whom ninety
' out of the hundred were to make their way
' in commercial life; but such was the fashion
' of the time.   By some favour, I was admitted
' a year or so ere I ought to have been.   No
' favour did it prove to me, so far as happiness
' was concerned; for, being the smallest, most
' nervous creature in the place, inexpert at
' every game, and shabbily dressed, being also
' credited with some quickness, I was a good
' deal plagued and rudely treated by the elder
' boys, not so much disliked as cruelly teazed,
' and in great difficulties as to the finding
' a playmate or a comrade.   To this day of
' writing, I wake up from a sort of nightmare
' dream that I am going to school, and have
' not my exercise ready.   There was a second
' master there, a Rev. Mr. Heathcote, who, I

' think, liked me.   I know I liked to learn
' from him, because he once set me on a stool
' in the middle of the school, to read aloud a
' theme which had pleased him—the only time
' such a distinction was paid a scholar in his
' room during my stay there.   This was a
' hard business to get through, and made me
' no more popular, of course, than I had been
' among my schoolfellows.   I learned Greek
' with greater relish than Latin.   The grandeur
' of the older language and of its poetry
' excited me, as compared with the smoother
' beauty of the tongue in which Cicero and .
' Virgil wrote.   To this day, too, I recollect
' the pleasure I found (when I was not idle) in
' Herodotus and in Euripides, whose "Hecuba"
' I translated from beginning to end, for my
' own pleasure.   At the school of the Royal
' Institution, when I first went there, corporeal
' punishment was forbidden.   Tasks to be got
' by heart were a light punishment to me,
' whose memory was then singularly alert and
' retentive.   And, in truth, I was learning
' things not fit for me, nor I for them ; and feel-

' ing, even then (for so I had been told) that the
' end of what I was learning was to be a desk
' in an American merchant's counting-house,
' I was, in every sense of the word—to myself,
' to my masters, to my schoolfellows, and at
' home—a failure : as such, too much taken to
' task, not enough coerced, and groping all the
' while towards a world in which there were
' neither Greek plays nor Latin orators, still
' less counting-house desks and ledgers. It was
' a time of weariness, and vain longing, and
' disapprobation, for which no one concerned
' was wholly to blame. With the habits, the
' traditions, and the views of all around me,
' there was no possibility of my having had
' the education for the art I have always loved
' the best. In those days, and in that place,
' a musician was hardly a man.

' But propensity, like murder, " will out," let
' the barriers be ever so intricate or unfriendly.
' There was a small music shop on our way to
' school ; there was an organ-building factory
' on another way back from it. By this time,
' I had been allowed a certain access to the

' pianoforte at home, pertinacity having pre-
' vailed ; and the readiness with which I picked
' out and picked up tunes was produced to
' such visitors as were not too severely bound
' to Quakerism to reject music. My uncle, too,
' had taken at one time an active part in the
' administration of the Blind Asylum, the
' musical pupils of which sang twice in the
' week—always sacred music—accompanied
' by an organ.   The selection of this was not
' bad, since fragments of Haydn, Mozart,
' Handel, and Pergolesi were included in it,
' as well as anthems by our later cathedral
' writers; and countless hymns. But that Blind
' School was my place of delight, and many
' and many a time have I lagged and loitered
' on my way to my school, to creep in there
' and hear something—certain, that whatever
' my excuse, I should be punished for my
' truancy.

' How I got into the music shop I have not
' the most remote idea ; but it belonged to good-
' natured people ; and the daughter of the
' house had been trained as a mistress of the

' pianoforte, and allowed me to hear her play
' sometimes — the first professionally-trained
' playing I had heard. In those days, "Der
' Freischütz" was new, and Kalkbrenner in
' the ascendant as a composer ; and his varia-
' tions on the "Hunting Chorus" (where are
' they now ?) were the things which Miss
' Walker had to get up, in order to teach her
' pupils. Long, too, ere I could have played
' them, I put together and wrote down a set
' of quadrille-tunes, which I had absolutely
' the assurance to present to these patient folk,
' with the hope of getting published. Their
' patience seems to me wonderful now.

' But I had more help in another quarter,
' strange to say, for which I was indebted to my
' uncle the physician, who despised music as a
' profession to such a point that I verily think
' he would rather have seen me a shop-boy than
' a second Mozart ! He was much beloved and
' trusted by his patients ; and no wonder, for
' he was as unselfish as he was sedulous. I
' could recall a hundred stories of his delicacy
' and disinterestedness : of his returning money

‘ when he considered himself over-feed; of his
‘ refusing it from patients in narrow circum-
‘ stances. Hence, the invalids who were in his
‘ hands for any length of time grew, most of
‘ them, to be his attached and grateful personal
‘ friends ; and some showed their attachment
‘ and gratitude in paying attention to his
‘ younger widowed sister and her four queer
‘ children.

‘ Among these was a woman of some wealth,
‘ who had married an Irish officer (of the old
‘ Bath or fortune-hunting species) some years
‘ younger than herself. They had four chil-
‘ dren, three of whom became insane, and died
‘ early; and, in the education of their daughter,
‘ they had called in a governess from London.
‘ She was Italian, or rather Nizzard, by birth,
‘ belonging to Mentone, in Sardinia ; and her
‘ father, she used to say, had been secretary to
‘ M. de Calonne, the well-known French
‘ minister. How this man, during the emigra-
‘ tion consequent on the Terror in Paris, could
‘ have obliged Georgiana, the brilliant Whig
‘ Duchess of Devonshire, it would be hard to

' tell. I have surmised (but it is mere surmise)
' that he might have been somehow convenient
' to her in the gambling transactions by which,
' it has been said, she suffered so much; but
' certain it is, the political beauty paid her
' debts to the man. by giving his daughter a
' first-class education, so as to fit her for earning
' her livelihood as a governess; and she was
' thereby installed in a Liverpool household.
' A woman with blue eyes, very black hair,
' the whitest skin I ever saw, and rather deaf;
' with a suspicious, self-defensive temper, but
' many real affections and sterling qualities,
' and more accomplishments, of a certain sort,
' than I had till then fallen in with. She was
' a true and solid pianoforte player, and (again
' good-natured) was willing to play for me
' sonatas by Dussek and Clementi, an arrange-
' ment of Cherubini's Overture to " Lodoiska,"
' and Beethoven's *Andante* in F for the piano-
' forte : so many introductions into Faëry land.
' In those days, I would have run miles
' through the rain to look at the outside of an
' organ. While we were living at St. Helens,

' I had been taken to church once or twice, and
' had heard what manner of rich and pompous
' sounds those noble instruments can give forth.
' Even such comfort and decoration as the
' church at St. Helens showed—seen by way of
' a change and a rarity—had early impressed
' me. To this day I never see an organ-front
' without that sort of expectation with which
' one gets near a mountain-top from which the
' view is known to be wide, or opens a green-
' house door to get a feast of colour and
' odour.

' It seems curious, that many persons should
' have agreed to mistake the love of colour for
' a frivolous passion for finery, and not have
' recognised that the eye has its satisfactions as
' complete as those that the ear derives from
' music or from sweet verse. All my earlier
' life I sat under the reproach of personal cox-
' combry and vanity, because I was born with
' a love of gay and harmonious tints, and of
' rich textures, and because I have loved to
' wear them, for their sakes—not for mine. I
' cannot recollect the period or the place at

' which I ever for one instant troubled my
' mind with the ridiculous notion of fascinating
' others by my fine clothes, or of passing off
' plain and irregular features by showy dress-
' ing. It has been my fortune, in common with
' other persons whose occupation makes them
' obnoxious, to receive much anonymous abuse,
' and to receive many of those singular counsels
' which careless people, not thinking themselves ill-natured, have as singular a pleasure
' in repeating, to see how the listener " takes
' " them." I can truly say, that I never, from
' my boyhood upwards, felt in the slightest
' degree ruffled or disconcerted by what seems
' to vex other less sensitive people than myself.
' Yet the ruling passion for blue, and rose-
' colour, and yellow, worn about me and upon
' me, broke out from the hour when I had a
' sixpence to call my own; and I still laugh, as
' I laughed then, at the ridicule showered upon
' me by my mates in Cropper, Benson and Co.'s
' office, when a half-starved tailor, whom I had
' commissioned to scour Liverpool for me in
' search of a cherry-coloured silk waistcoat,

' presented himself at the cash-keeper's counter
' of that busy establishment, with a pattern for
' Mr. Chorley, which he hoped "would do, at
" ' last."

  ' So, too, in my fancies for drawing,—and I
' had till I was a grown man some fancy, but
' no learning ;—it was the arabesque—the rich
' and decorative composition—in which I de-
' lighted; the high finish of miniature paint-
' ing, the most crimson sunsets of landscape.
' There may have been something of very low
' artistic feeling, or instinct, or sensuality in
' all this—a something linked with tastes and
' tendencies for another art which were of
' higher quality. I do not believe in a gift for
' poetry without some developed or undeveloped
' capacity for painting, music, or *vice versâ.* A
' musician I should have been; and since the
' technical training and the opportunities of
' self-culture were denied me by circumstance,
' secondary talents grouped around the central
' one, which were more easily indulged and de-
' veloped, broke out as it were, to satisfy a
' want which must find some relief. Thus, I

' drew (I ought to say, coloured) patiently, for
' hours upon hours; and the slowest, most ela-
' borate, most tedious works.   I—who was the
' idlest of boys at my books, the most restless
' of creatures, living or dead, in what is
' thought improving company—have got up in
' the middle of the night, to see whether I had
' spoiled the yesterday's work.   I rose habitu-
' ally for some years (always a reluctant riser)
' with daylight, that I might pursue my favour-
' ite occupation for some hours before I betook
' myself to the abominable school or the detest-
' able counting-house; and there were long ex-
' tant, acres, I may say, of ill-devised, ill-consi-
' dered essays at colour, in fruit, flower, land-
' scape pieces, and sometimes heads in minia-
' ture, which might have told those in care of
' me that I had industry and labour to bestow,
' and earnest diligence under command and
' control, in the objects and pursuits which
' really interested me.   But who thinks of these
' things with regard to children except those
' who themselves have some sympathy with the
' artist-temperament?   My mother possessed

' it, but did not know it. There were glimpses
' of it, too, in my father's family. But those
' were days when, in the provinces of Eng-
' land, to get recognition or respect for tastes or
' fancies of the kind I speak of, required more
' than ordinary courage and foresight on the
' part of parents and guardians. Mine, though
' gifted, were timid, narrowed in fortunes, and
' full of the Nonconformist horror of Art, as a
' calling, which existed so strangely among
' those who were quick enough to relish art as
' an amusement.

' It seems to me now, in putting together all
' these revelations, that had my elders under-
' stood the signs before them, and apprenticed
' me to a musical career, I might have done
' England an artist's service. But I hardly
' know the middle-class family in the provinces
' forty years ago (save, perhaps, one so much
' before its age, as that of the Taylors of Nor-
' wich), where such a disposition of a boy's life
' would not then have been considered as a de-
' gradation. How the good people of those
' days resigned themselves to going to theatres

' and music-meetings, I have never been able to
' understand, even on the most comprehensive
' theory of inconsistency. I know that my
' wings were perpetually breaking against the
' cage, and that unable to get out, as I wished,
' I had to make other outlets for humour, or
' taste, or talent which *would not* conform to
' the life chalked out for me. I wanted plea-
' sure, sympathy, scope for the fancy; and I
' loved and looked up to people, in proportion
' as they could minister these to me. No crea-
' ture in prison was ever more resolute than I
' was to get out. But long and weary was the
' time ere extrication came; and when it did
' come, it was only, as it were, along a by-
' road.'

CHAPTER III.

Impression of character derived from Chorley's Journals—
Enters a merchant's office in Liverpool—Distasteful em-
ployment—Literary and artistic tastes—Intimacy with
Mr. Rathbone, and its influence on his life—Early efforts
in literature—Mrs. Procter's reminiscences—Society in
Liverpool—Mrs. Hemans—American merchant captains
and their wives—Cultivation of music and critical taste
—Mr. Gnosspelius' reminiscences—Instruction by J. Z.
Herrmann — Associates — M. Grisar — Introduction to
'Athenæum'—Opening of Liverpool and Manchester
Railway—Letter to Mr. Dilke—Contributions to 'Athe-
næum'—Application to be admitted on staff accepted—
Arrival in London—Literary criticism—Letter to a friend
in Liverpool—Letter from Mr. Dilke.

At this point a chasm occurs in Chorley's
Autobiography, which must be filled up from
other sources. One of the chief of these is
the series of his journals, which extends (with
breaks of considerable duration) from 1827 to
1852. They are marked "private;" and

throughout convey a sense of being genuine soliloquies, written under immediate impulse, at moments when a man is least likely to be deceived as to his own feelings. No more trustworthy index of character is probably ever obtainable than memorials of this description. After as impartial a study of these as I have been able to make, the impression derived of the writer's moral personality is, that he was naturally endowed with rare simplicity, purity, sincerity, warm affections, refined sensibility, and buoyant enthusiasm—gifts which were only alloyed by their conjunction with tendencies to self-assertion and impatience, and their embodiment in an unhealthy *physique*. Such an organisation might be expected to prove susceptible to change for better or for worse in favourable or unfavourable conditions; and the deteriorating effect of circumstance upon the writer's mind is painfully apparent as these records proceed. Under the influence of habitual loneliness and ill-health, repeated disappointment, misconstruction, and failure,

he becomes morbidly sensitive, more pronounced in self-assertion, often irritable and
querulous; but he is for ever struggling
against these tendencies, and deploring his
weakness in yielding to them. His enthusiasm for Art, and the high standard of honour
whereby he " magnifies his office," supply
constant correctives; and to the last his heart
remains unaltered, ever prompt to generous
motives, and kindling under a breath of sympathy. Few readers of these journals, I
think, could fail to respect and pity the writer
of them; and those who had most reason, in
after years, to quarrel with his eccentricities
of disposition, would here discern the cause, and
accord him forgiveness. That the foregoing
impression of Chorley's moral characteristics
is well-founded, I have the best reason for
believing, in that the self-portraiture conveyed
by his journals completely tallies with my own
observation of him, which extends from the
year 1861 to the date of his death.

What light these memorials throw upon his
intellectual life will best appear from the ex-

tracts made from them. Hastily written as they are, their rough draughts of the impressions which his mind received—whether from active contact with an original genius, or passive observation of natural or artistic beauty and social manners—have often a freshness that his more finished descriptions want; while those critical and dramatic faculties, the display of which in his published works has sometimes a semblance of artificial elaboration, are here seen at their ease in undress.

Thus much it has seemed desirable to say by way of introductory reference to the sources from which a great part of this narrative will be drawn; but the estimate attempted has been of necessity prospective, and its justification will not be immediately apparent. The opening scenes of Chorley's career present such features only as are calculated to awaken the reader's interest and admiration. Whatever regret may be occasioned by the spectacle of youthful aspiration thwarted by untoward fortune, and the shortsightedness of

those who should have discerned and fostered
a talent that, for want of such providence,
fell short of its full development, will but
heighten respect for the energy and courage
which, in spite of all obstacles, contrived to
achieve so much.

The unmistakable indications in the boy's
temperament and habits of an artistic bias,
which should have determined his career,
were—however inevitably and excusably—
wholly disregarded by his family; and,
at an early age, he was taken from school,
and assigned to a clerkship in the office
of Messrs. Cropper, Benson and Co., a prosperous firm of American merchants in Liverpool. How long he remained there does not
appear; but, the occupation not being to his
liking, he was transferred to a seat in the office
of Messrs. Woodhouse, Sicilian wine-growers.
The result was the same. An employment
more thoroughly distasteful to him than the
checking of invoices and casting up of ledgers
could scarcely have been chosen; and he
appears to have performed his duties quite

perfunctorily, without any interest but the
hope of escape into a more congenial atmosphere. To shorten the hours of official
drudgery as much as possible, and secure
every available opportunity of indulging his
love of Art, especially music, of literature,
and society, was his constant and increasingly
eager aim. In the culture and gratification
of these tastes he was warmly encouraged by
the sympathy and assisted by the liberality
of Mr. Benson Rathbone, the son of the lady
whose early kindness he has affectionately
recorded. The companionship of a man so
much older than himself, of maturer mind and
ampler means, was invaluable to Chorley at this
crisis of his life. His visits to Swansea and
Geldeston—where Mr. Rathbone successively
resided, and gave his young friend opportunities of hearing and practising music—
were seasons of rare enchantment to him. It
is probable, too, that his introduction to the
Italian Opera in London was made under
the same auspices. The cost of a journey
thither from Liverpool was far too great

for him to have undertaken it unassisted; and it seems likely that the visits which he speaks of having paid there before 1834, were in Mr. Rathbone's company. A grateful remembrance of this gentleman's timely sympathy remained with Chorley to the close of his life; and the shadow cast over his brightening prospects by his friend's premature death, a few years later, was not lightly lifted. The period of their friendship, between 1827 and 1834, was that of Chorley's first literary efforts. Sketches of character and manners drawn from his observation of Liverpool life; tales, lyrics and hymns; a dramatic poem, of which Stradella was the hero; and sundry criticisms on music—of which more will presently be said —were the fruit of such moments as could be snatched from the desk. A few of these productions appeared in the " Winter's Wreath," the " Sacred Offering," and other of the annual collections of verse and prose then popular (to which his mother and sister, and both his brothers, were also contributors); and a larger number in the minor serials; some of his songs, also, being set to music.

A personal reminiscence of him at this period has been kindly furnished by Mrs. Procter, the wife of Mr. Bryan Procter (Barry Cornwall). She remembers Chorley coming to the house of her father (Mr. Basil Montagu) in London, about the year 1830, accompanied by Archdeacon Wrangham, a friend of the family, who asked permission to bring him to breakfast. Chorley impressed her as a romantic, enthusiastic youth, plain-featured, with red hair; his manner gentlemanly, but marked by the same nervous timidity that he retained to the last, and a touch of Quaker quaintness—the result of early association—that he soon dropped, which greatly interested Mr. Montagu, who was much attached to the sect. The acquaintance thus formed was renewed when Chorley came up to town in 1834, and ripened into a friendship that remained uninterrupted till death.

Apart from its association with his detested drudgery, a seaport like Liverpool—teeming with various and ever-changing forms of activity, the residence of merchant princes, and the temporary abode of strangers attracted thither by diverse motives from all parts of the globe—was not an ungenial soil for the development of such tastes and ambitions as his. The circle of society in which he mixed was more than ordinarily cultivated, and frequently received additions which gave it fresh colour and interest. One of these was Mrs. Hemans, who resided in the neighbourhood of Liverpool for some years, and whose poetic prestige and personal influence inspired Chorley with a reverence of which the traces are apparent, not only in the imitative manner of his early verses, but in a pervading want of manliness in the fibre of his thought, which the stern training of his after-experience was needful to supply. Another and very different addition to his social circle, but scarcely less welcome from the stimulus it afforded to his love of character, was the succession of American merchant-captains who were frequent guests at the tables to

which he was invited.   Of this type of visitor
he has left the following pleasant reminiscence.

‘ I think of them as a fine, hearty, whole-
‘ some race of seafaring men; in general
‘ breeding and intelligence superior to any-
‘ thing analogous of home-growth which Liver-
‘ pool could have produced. They brought an
‘ air, sometimes a gale, of freshness into a
‘ society which, in those days, was restricted,
‘ and, therefore, given up to struggles and
‘ demarcations of petty class insolence, happily
‘ now over for ever. They had strange sea-
‘ stories to tell—sometimes with a rich allow-
‘ ance of *braggadocio*—sometimes, in the abund-
‘ ance of that restlessness which is so marking
‘ a feature in the national character. They
‘ brought over their wives to have a good time
‘ of it, by way of a frolic; and as a class,
‘ jolly, hearty, and original these wives were—
‘ fond of display—fond of indulgence—strange
‘ in their speech; but in no case that I can
‘ recollect unwomanly, or breaking those innate
‘ laws of good breeding which do not depend

' on orthodox speech or minute subservience
' to any code of ceremonies.

' One of these cheery beings especially lives
' in my recollection, who was deservedly made
' much of in Liverpool, and who passed many
' an evening by our fireside, which her presence
' brightened. She dressed richly. I see as
' clearly as if nearly half a century had not
' passed, a certain orange robe of Canton crape,
' and the gold chain across her forehead, orna-
' mented in the centre, as was the fashion then,
' by a *feronniere*. Those who have seen the sadly
' speaking portrait of Malibran will know what
' I mean. That was a mere jewel drop, worn,
' as I have seen an orange-flower bud in Spain,
' so as just to hang beneath the parting of the
' hair. But, whereas other ladies indulged in
' blossoms or pendants, dear Mrs. —— had
' bethought herself of a small French watch,
' the hands of which went round, and which
' ticked in an excruciating manner.'

Most attractive to him of all the advantages
of Liverpool life, were such means as it provided for the gratification of his thirst for

music. The 'first public music of any kind' which he heard was, as he notes in his journal, at the Liverpool Festival of 1827. This introduced him to Mozart's "Jupiter Symphony," from which, although 'at that time ' far from being able to receive anything more ' than a vague impression of delight,' he derived such an impression as 'amounted to ' ecstasy.' Here, too, he heard Pasta, of whom his critical estimate, as the earliest of a life-long series, may be worth quoting. 'The ' first tones of her voice quite shocked me; ' there was a coarse huskiness about them ' which made wild work with my pre-conceived ' ideas of nightingale sweetness and the other ' fantasies of an uneducated brain about sing-' ers; but the song was "Ombra Adorata,"* and ' though I have heard many good and inspired ' things since, her *reading* of that melody stands ' out distinct from anything I have ever heard; ' the perfection of passion controlled by dig-' nity, of high resolve sustained by higher hope. ' It has left an impression of majesty and

* From the " Romeo" of Zingarelli.

' first-rate talent which I cannot fancy any
' new pleasure will efface.' The same journal
recounts his first attendance at a stage representation, and hearing of Italian opera—the
piece being Rossini's "Il Turco in Italia,"
which was given by a company that visited
Liverpool for a short season, with 'Spag-
' noletti for leader; Fanny Ayton, *prima*
' *donna*; Curioni, tenor; Giubilei and De
' Begnis, *serio* and *buffo* basses.' A visit which
was paid to Liverpool, in 1832, by Donzelli,
then among the first of Italian tenors, further
enlarged Chorley's experience both of operatic
and sacred music; and he dilates in his
journal, with boyish enthusiasm, on the rapture
with which he had listened. 'I would go a
' mile to hear Donzelli sing his scales. It is
' the only voice I ever heard wherein extreme
' power existed without a shadow of strain or
' shout; . . . and there is appertaining to
' and beyond these mere animal gifts, a soul,
' a nice delicacy of taste, a quiet sobriety in
' the choice of ornament, a regulated passion
' (how far stronger than the false frenzy of

' many artists!) which heightens the impres-
' sion his voice produces to the extremest point
' of pleasure.'

Between 1830 and 1833, Chorley's musical training was substantially strengthened by his becoming enrolled in a society of *amateurs* which had recently been established in Liverpool. For the following particulars of this association I am indebted to the kindness of a surviving member, one of his oldest friends, Mr. Gnosspelius.

"The first opportunity Chorley had of hearing and taking part in chamber music, was as member of a small musical society of *amateurs*, of whom very few are now left, but who were all full of genuine love of the art. The meetings were held at the houses of the members, and nowhere did he feel himself more at home than in the house of Mr. Fletcher (the banker), of whose handsome and accomplished daughters the eldest, Harriett, and the youngest, Louisa, were especial favourites of his, and continued his firm friends to the end of their noble and self-sacrificing lives. Samuel Kearsley, a well-known Liverpool musical enthusiast, and his talented wife also belonged to the same society, and with them Chorley continued his intimate friendship as long as they lived.

" From 1830 to 1833, he acted as secretary to this society; and the good-humoured way in which he smoothed down the feelings of ambition and small jealousy, from which few young *amateurs* are wholly free, was long remembered by the members, who were mainly kept together by his unceasing activity—an activity the success of which, he often said, proved that the duties of an *impresario* would by no means be too much for him."

Another and a prominent member of this society was Mrs. Ambrose Lace, to whom Chorley subsequently dedicated the first work which he wrote in connection with the art. Mr. Gnosspelius remembers this lady as " in those days, perhaps the most attractive amongst the ladies of Liverpool," and that Chorley was greatly aided by her " in his early

struggles for emancipation from the drudgery
of an office and for introduction into society
more congenial to him than that of Quaker-
dom." To the professional teacher of this
band of *amateurs*, the late James Z. Herrmann,
afterwards conductor of the Liverpool Philharmonic Society, Chorley was indebted for
the only systematic teaching in music which
I believe he ever received. Of this gentleman, Mr. Gnosspelius recalls that he was "the
leader of that German quartette who, in 1829,
under the name of Gebrüder Herrmann, came
to England, and first introduced genuine
quartette-playing to the English public. Settled
in Liverpool early in 1830, J. Z. Herrmann
soon began to lay the foundation of that better
taste for music, which has since taken root
there, to a degree most remarkable to those
who remember that then there were only two
ladies in the whole town who could attempt
a Beethoven *sonata*. How much he owed
to Herrmann, Chorley was always ready to
acknowledge. Meanwhile, though his zeal in
benefiting by his friend's instruction was at

first great, it soon became evident that anything like executive proficiency was not to be attained by him, and this he had the good sense to acknowledge. The pianoforte parts of a couple of trios by Hummel, and a quartette of Beethoven, were all that his indulgent master induced him to attempt; but they too often ended in a nervous breakdown."

Another of his musical associates at this period, M. Albert Grisar, offered a partial parallel to himself in his nascent tastes and future career. From a little notice of his death, which Chorley wrote in the 'Athenæum' of June 26, 1869, I extract the following :—

'The idea of his parents was to make of ' him a man of business, and with this purpose ' he was sent to Liverpool and placed in a ' merchant's office, somewhere about the year ' 1830. There I came to know him and to ' see completely that nothing in the shape of ' merchandise would satisfy the spirit of a ' man who craved and would have another life

' than the life of ledgers and duplicate letters.
' After a short period of enforced and un-
' willing servitude, having expressed through-
' out tendencies rather than talents for music,
' he somehow broke away and got home.
' The next thing that was to be heard of
' Grisar was, that he had planted his foot on
' the musical ladder, by his gaining accept-
' ance, in the year 1836, at the " Opera
' " Comique " of Paris (no easy matter), for an
' operetta, &c.'

Here the fortunes of the two men diverged. Grisar became a popular writer of comic operas for the Parisian stage; Chorley, a man of letters, and only a librettist and song-writer in the world of art for which he was best fitted.

During 1832 and 1833, a succession of musical and dramatic treats — hearings of Beethoven's " Fidelio," Rossini's " Otello," Mozart's " Nozze," Handel's " Israel " and " Messiah," Haydn's " Creation " and " 2nd Mass," Mozart's " Requiem " and " 12th Credo," and Spohr's " Last Judgment,"—of

Schroeder-Devrient, and Malibran—gave a fresh stimulus to Chorley's growing faculty of discernment. The accounts in his journal of each representation that he attended became less rhapsodical and more discriminative. He was evidently feeling his way to a definite vocation.

Mr. Gnosspelius' reminiscences include an interesting illustration of Chorley's consciousness of his own power.

"On hearing his brother John and myself speak with delight of certain musical criticisms of the German humourist, Hoffmann, he asked me, as he had no knowledge of German, to translate for him two chapters from the 'Phantasienstücke' (if I remember right, 'An Evening with Kapellmeister Kreisler' and 'A Critique on Don Juan'); and I well remember the exultation with which he exclaimed, on reading the translation, 'That is what *I* can do, and what I *will* do.' In these few words, the story of his life seems to be compressed."

The suggestion which led to his obtaining

such an opportunity as he desired, Chorley owed, I believe, to the elder Miss Jewsbury (afterwards Mrs. Fletcher), in her time a popular authoress, with whom he had become acquainted in Liverpool. She was an early contributor to the 'Athenæum,' then rising in public estimation, under the vigorous management of Charles Wentworth Dilke, as a formidable rival to the 'Literary Gazette,' which, under the sway of Jerdan, had long wielded a stern despotism over current literature and art. At her instance it would seem that, in September, 1830, Mr. Dilke applied to Chorley, as a young Liverpool penman, for an account of the ceremony that was to inaugurate the new railway between that town and Manchester. The accident which caused the death of the eminent statesman, Huskisson, imparted a tragic interest to an event which would otherwise have been solely memorable in the unemotional annals of Science, and Chorley felt that no worthy narrative of the occasion could omit to call attention to its twofold significance. But he found himself unable to do justice to the subject in its scientific aspect, and was candid enough to say so.   Under date of September 22nd, 1830, he thus wrote to Mr. Dilke :—

" DEAR SIR,

    "I received your very obliging letter of the 18th and the ' Athenæum ' for Sunday last upon Monday morning. I have delayed answering it till to-day, because I was anxious, if possible, to prove to you that I meant what I said when I offered you my services, and to have sent you such an article as you wished. But after one or two ineffectual efforts, I became convinced anew, of what past experience might have taught me, that I am incapable of writing anything *scientific*, and that I could do little but extract from Encyclopædias, &c. In fact, the trifle you receive with this (of which I beg your acceptance, though it is rather like giving a stone for a fish), may show you that I have lived more among the romance than the reality of literature. What I purposed to have sent you would have been a light sketch of the proceedings of the day, with perhaps a grain of information among a mass of nonsense—'a halfpenny worth of bread to an intolerable quantity of sack.' It may seem ridiculous, and I fear disobliging, to have troubled you, and after all to be of no use; but I have seen and laughed at so much grave folly perpetrated by those who have been unwise enough to forsake their own peculiar line, that I have made a kind of resolution never to put on the lion's skin for fear, lest my asses' ears should be too long to be hidden. If I can at any time serve you with lighter contributions of prose or verse, I shall be most happy; or if you should at any time like to have any *musical* papers, I think I could undertake to promise you my best efforts, as I love the art dearly, and have spent much time in its cultivation. I ought to apologise for having intruded upon your time so long, but I was anxious that you should understand me thoroughly, in case you should be disposed to avail yourself of my services on any future occasion. In the meantime, I remain,

> "Your obedient servant,
> "Henry F. Chorley.

"14, St. Anne Street."

Mr. Dilke appears to have appreciated this candour, and sent a favourable answer; whereupon Chorley forwarded several lyrics, and one or two musical criticisms, which were duly inserted. His earliest critical effort, according to his recollection, 'was an account ' of the quaint Musical Festival in Dublin, ' when Paganini was compelled to mount on ' the case of the grand pianoforte, and exhibit ' his gaunt face and spectral proportions while ' he played.'

The acceptance of these contributions decided Chorley's career. Towards the close of 1833, by the intervention of a Quaker acquaintance, Mr. Pringle, the African traveller, he applied to Mr. Dilke for admission on the staff of the journal, expressing himself willing to accept a salary commencing at 80*l.* a year.

The conditions of assent prescribed in Mr. Dilke's straightforward answer were severe enough to have daunted an ordinary aspirant. "I would consent to take my chance," he wrote, "of your being more or less useful to me, and would give you 50*l. for six months' services.* This would enable you to take up a position here, and at least to maintain you, according to your own estimate, while you waited on fortune, and further and better employment. In return, I should require you to live in my *immediate neighbourhood;* and to give me your assistance in any and every way I might suggest. It may, indeed, be presumed that I mean to shift from my shoulders to yours *as much of the drudgery as possible,* being heartily weary of it. I cannot say how much of your time I should require, because that would depend on your facility and despatch. I am, however, of opinion that at least one whole day a week would be at your disposal, and perhaps some hours of one or two other days. Nor would your occupation be *always* disagreeable; but as much of it would be to *rewrite* papers—a wearisome business, as I know—I think it better to declare at once that it will be generally *drudgery*."

Chorley responded to this offer by accepting it " with pleasure and without hesitation." 'I was resolved,' he says in a fragment of autobiography, ' to be delivered from Liver- ' pool, where no occupation presented itself, ' save such as I detested, and the duties of ' which I fulfilled as imperfectly as possible. ' The remuneration offered to a person so un- ' tried was naturally very small. The idea, I ' suspect, was to entrust me with nothing of ' consequence or involving responsibility; but ' I would have taken service on any terms to ' escape from the intolerable drudgery of a ' merchant's office. I concealed the conditions ' of my engagement from my family, aware ' that they had no confidence in my stability ' of purpose. It was believed by them that I ' should return home, after a time of failure, ' in debt. The parting, when it came, was ' less bitter to my kith and kin than to

' myself, because of this apprehension on their
' part.

    ' I . left Liverpool on the last day of
' the year 1833, going *viâ* Manchester, and
' thence outside a coach, which, it seems now
' inconceivable, was six-and-twenty hours
' on the road. The weather was of the very
' worst winter kind; the horses could hardly
' make head against a storm of wind, which,
' as we passed through Derbyshire, blew
' over a worse-appointed stage-coach before
' us. It snowed heavily, and my hat was
' blown off. The bitter cold at dawn of that
' new year's day is a thing never to be for-
' gotten; and when I arrived at my destina-
' tion (Mr. Dilke having kindly invited me to
' his house till I could establish myself), I
' was numb, stupid, hardly able to speak, to
' think, or to move. I have been told, that
' early in the evening I was found fast asleep,
' having fallen out of the fire-side chair, where
' the most warm-hearted of hostesses had kindly
' placed me, with my head in the coal-scuttle.
' I feel—even at this distance of time — my

' state of intense and shabby misery, of ache,
' and pain, and exhaustion, when I woke.
' But it was something to begin a man's life in
' London, and during the early months of my
' probation (some of which were anything
' but light ones, involving the most rigorous
' economy) I never, for an instant, repented
' the step I had taken, which even the most
' indulgent of my friends—to whose kindness
' and trust in me I was largely indebted—felt
' and feared was rash, one not improbably in-
' volving ruin for life.

' Matters were not mended by my intense
' and awkward shyness. It was well that my
' employers, and a correspondent or two, had
' received a not unfavourable idea of me from
' the few slight contributions to annuals and
' magazines which I had published. By those
' among whom I was thrown by chance—a
' *coterie*, not devoid of *coterie* self-conceit, and
' sharply intolerant—I was viewed with little
' favour; and when it appeared that I was
' about to stand my ground, I was not kindly
' treated as an interloper.'

Having settled himself in a modest lodging, No. 5, Stafford Row, Pimlico, he commenced his career as a man of letters on the slender basis of connection with a single journal. The work entrusted to him was sufficiently varied, as is attested by the list which he has preserved of his contributions; nor can it be doubted that an estimate more than ordinarily high must have been formed of his ability, before a youth thus untried would have been chosen by so shrewd a judge as Mr. Dilke to sit in judgment upon authors with an established reputation, such as Moore, Landor, Southey, Crabbe, Mrs. Hemans, William and Mary Howitt, and Mrs. Jameson, and to write the obituary notice of such a veteran as Coleridge. Among the works of writers then less distinguished, which were submitted to Chorley's verdict in the first year of his engagement on the ' Athenæum,' was the " Revolutionary Epic " of Mr. Disraeli. Besides reviews of books, he undertook, in part at least, the criticism of musical performances, operas, concerts, and festivals, and of the principal exhibitions of pictures and drawings.

A letter which he wrote, three months after his arrival in London, to Mrs. Richard Rathbone, one of his oldest friends in Liverpool, sums up the general result of his experience thus far.

" 5, Stafford Row, Pimlico.
"April 15, 1834.

" MY DEAR FRIEND,

"I was much obliged by your kind note, which reached me on Monday along with the week's parcel. I should, indeed, have written long ago, but you judge only rightly in concluding my engagements many; and were I not perforce thrown off my work by a man who is tuning my piano, I should not have had time to have answered yours before Saturday, that being my holiday, which, however, I have been too busy to claim for many a week. I am rather indisposed to desk-work, as you may suppose; and I thought you would hear of me by Mrs. R., to whom I write as my first friend in the family, save your mother, to whom only I

VOL. I. H

do not write because she must have letters enough to read without mine.

" It is a strange, confused, bustling life I am living, and were I much in society, I think I should go crazy; but I do not go out much beyond *duty*-visiting yet, nor, in fact, have I time, as I am rarely done before ten o'clock at night, and *never* if I take up any of my own private matters. But it is (as I expected) a life of great interest, and I feel I am of use, and filling my place creditably, which I never felt before; so that I am very happy, though it would have been hard to make some folks believe that I could be so, living as much alone as I do, and so constantly employed. My occupation, too, is all indoors work, and I never go abroad, save to see something *officially*, or on a constitutional walk. My chief recreation is the opera and evening concerts. Private music I hear none, and I think shall be almost entirely compelled to give up my own share of it, as I am not at the piano half an hour a day. My connection with the ' Athenæum ' continues all I could possibly wish *in every respect*. Had I sought all the

world over, I could not have found a situation
more to my mind. My book is rapidly going
through the press, . . . and I have every
prospect of an arrangement for another, when
I have time to write it. My 'Seaport Town'
will be out about the middle of June, I believe. . . . I have seen abundance of the
lions of literature here, and my respect for
them has by no means increased. . . . The
Procters, however, I like much. . . . I think
Hood, perhaps, the most taking lion I have
seen, perhaps because he does not try to take,
and his wit comes out really because it cannot
stop in, there is so much behind. . . . I met
Mr. Atherstone* (for the first time) on
Sunday evening, who contradicted everything
that six people said as fast as they could say
it; but he says he is starving for his health,
and that I know, by lean experience, is enough
to make any one cross, let alone a poet. . . .
You have no taste for *spectacle*, or I would
tell you that the Opera is more magnificent

* The then famous author of the " Fall of Nineveh."—
(H. G. H.)

than ever, and a certain Mademoiselle Grisi the best of best singers. . . . Will you give my dear love to your mother? I think of her often, and always with affection and gratitude. I am sure she will rejoice with me at such an apparently prosperous termination of long indecision and unsettlement. . . . My love to all the children. I hope you hear pleasant tidings of H. M. Believe me to be yours faithfully,

"HENRY F. CHORLEY."

The satisfaction thus expressed with his employment was reciprocated by his employer, as appears from the following letter, addressed to him by Mr. Dilke, on the termination of their six months' engagement :—

"1st July, 1834.
"MY DEAR SIR,

"It has just struck me to ask you how our accounts stand? I think you have had 40*l.*; but, unfortunately, my son does not appear to have made any entry of the last amount paid. On this *supposition*, I enclose a draft for 14*l.*; 4*l.* being added for articles on Dublin Musical Festival, &c. . . . And now a word about the future, of which I ought, perhaps, to have spoken before, but that I am not an observer of dates, until quarter-day knocks at the door with all amiable remembrances. I think I may be brief on this subject. I am very well satisfied with your zeal and ability to serve the paper, especially when thoroughly broken into harness; and I don't think you find much to object to in your position. What say you, then, if I give you 65*l. for the next six months*, it being understood between us, as heretofore, that I mean to thrust all the drudgery on you that I can, according to conscience? This may be a little more than it has been, but principally in sight-seeing, as I have upon occasion intimated; but, in fact, you know now what it is likely to be, as well as I do.

" I am, my dear Sir,

" Yours very truly,

" C. W. DILKE.

"I send half a dozen volumes for L. T. ['Library Table'], this or next week, as may suit."

The arrangement proposed was frankly accepted by Chorley in his reply. It deserves to be noted here, that out of the first money which he earned in his new vocation, he repaid the sums which certain of his friends in Liverpool had lent him to defray his immediate expenses. This punctuality was the more honourable to him that these friends were not in a position to need, and would never have pressed for repayment.

Henceforward his life was divided pretty equally between the claims of literature and Art, what was left being absorbed in attention to those of friendship and society. In place therefore of attempting what it would be impossible to achieve—a consecutive and chronological narrative of his career as a whole, I shall endeavour to sketch it in each of the three aspects of literary, artistic, and social life, which it from this time assumed.

CHAPTER IV.

CHORLEY'S connection with the ' Athenæum ' continued unbroken till a few years before his death, and formed, in fact, his only permanent occupation. Looking back upon it towards the close of life, he recalls with

pleasure that ' this prolonged period of ser-
' vice was accepted and accomplished with-
' out a single angry word or failure of obli-
' gation on either side.   I believe the secret of
' this to have been in the respect for punctu-
' ality maintained by both contracting parties.
' This, in the large sense of the word, implies
' honesty of speech, when speech is necessary,
' and integrity in dealing.   It does not include
' agreement in opinion, still less a subservience
' beyond the obligations which regulate the
' position of superior and subordinate.   No
' two persons could be more unlike in many
' matters of taste, opinion, and feeling than
' the editor of the " Athenæum," the late
' honoured Charles Dilke, and myself.   But it
' was impossible to know and not respect him,
' how ever so many were his prejudices (and
' they were many), how ever so limited were
' his sympathies (and they were limited).   That
' he had a similar feeling in regard to myself,
' I have reason to believe.'

The cheerful and healthy tone of this reminiscence must be set off against many

expressions of a more gloomy cast which follow. The relation subsisting between himself and Mr. Dilke, as their correspondence attests, was one of the most cordial intimacy ; and Chorley repeatedly expressed, in no stinted terms, his grateful sense of the kindness shown to him. The *couleur de rose* impression of a literary life, however, which pervades the foregoing letter to his friend in Liverpool, was, of course, merely transient. Though the "sweets and sours" were tolerably well mixed in his career as a whole, there would certainly seem to have been an undue proportion of the latter in the section of it which was devoted to literature. For some of his failures as an author there were reasons proper to himself and his themes, which sufficiently exonerated his readers from blame. The hostility that was excited by his criticism, on the other hand, can be accounted discreditable only to those who felt, not to him who caused it.

The prevailing spirit of his reviews at this period, so far as I am acquainted with them, whether of books, pictures, or music, seems to me singularly fair and generous. They are, no doubt, occasionally rigorous, but without a trace of flippancy, much less of truculence. The earlier ones are slight and inadequately discriminative, but year by year the writer's touch becomes sensibly finer, and his tone proportionally firmer. From first to last, a cordial sympathy with whatever he held to be true and noble in literature and art, and severity in his censure of whatever came short of this standard, characterised his discharge of the critical function entrusted to him, and amply justified the confidence expressed in his employer's letter. Nor was that confidence ever shaken by any outbreaks of dislike which were provoked by his strictures. Their fearless sincerity was thoroughly in keeping with the tone of a journal which had acquired its reputation for honesty by contrast with the 'Literary Gazette.' Such, at least, was Chorley's own opinion, as the following passage will show, though how far that opinion was influenced by the personal con-

siderations which he candidly avows in connection with it, I have no means of judging.

'At the time when I joined the " Athe-
' " næum," its vigour and value to the world of
' letters were not acknowledged as they have
' since been. The " Literary Gazette," con-
' ducted by Mr. Jerdan, who was the puppet of
' certain booksellers, and dispensed praise or
' blame at their bidding, and it may be feared
' " for a consideration," was in the ascendancy;
' and its conductors and writers spared no
' pains to attack, to vilipend, and to injure, so
' far as they could, any one who had to do with
' a rising journal so merciless in its exposure of
' a false and demoralising system.

' It would not be easy to sum up the ini-
' quities of criticism (the word is not too
' strong), perpetrated at the instance of pub-
' lishers, by a young writer and a woman, who
' was in the grasp of Mr. Jerdan, and who gilt
' or blackened all writers of the time, as he
' ordained. When I came to London to join
' the " Athenæum," she " was flinging about
' " fire " as a journalist in sport, according to

' the approved fashion of her school, and not a
' small quantity of the fire fell on the head of
' one who belonged to " the opposition" camp,
' like myself. It is hard to conceive any one,
' by flimsiness and by flippancy, made more
' distasteful to those who did not know her,
' than was Miss Landon.

' For years, the amount of gibing sarcasm
' and imputation to which I was exposed, was
' largely swelled by this poor woman's com-
' manded spite. That it did not make me
' seriously unhappy was probably an affair of
' temperament; those who would have been
' pained by it were, happily, beyond reach of
' hearing. But that these things most as-
' suredly had a bad influence on my power as
' a worker, I do not entertain the slightest
' doubt. Perhaps it is only the lingering
' vanity of an elderly man which I mistake
' for conviction.'

That the touch of rancour which may be
thought perceptible in this notice of Miss
Landon did not permanently affect Chorley's
estimate of her, nor steel his kindly nature

against her subsequent misfortunes, will be apparent from a later notice.

To some extent the obloquy which attached to him in certain quarters, on account of his connection with the 'Athenæum,' was reflected, being directly attributable to the doings of his colleagues, for whom he was a scapegoat. An instance in point is furnished in the following sketch of the staff of which he was a member :—' At that time ' (1834) the " Athenæum " was largely sup- ' ported, in point of contributions, by many of ' Mr. Dilke's former comrades in " The London ' " Magazine." Charles Lamb gave the journal ' some of his last and not least racy fragments. ' Hood, too, when he could be prevailed on to ' cast off the habits of procrastination which ' had so disturbing an effect on his fortunes, ' lent a hand from time to time; and some of ' his whimsical criticisms are not even to be ' surpassed by the best comicalities in his ' " Whims and Oddities." It must be an in- ' creasing object of regret to all who love that ' which is original or powerful in imaginative

' prose and verse, that Hood gave such small
' time and labour to the public. Though he
' used to profess that he could not control his
' demon, as an excuse for his indolence, a time
' always arrived when it became a matter of
' life and death, of daily and nightly toil, to
' hurry through the work, long contracted and
' largely paid for in advance. For years this
' amounted to nothing beyond the small an-
' nual volume of comic and grotesque fancies.

' Then, too, the " Athenæum " was from
' time to time enriched by Barry Cornwall's
' gem-like and musical verses, and by the
' brilliant, yet not always refined, criticisms
' of Hood's brother-in-law and partner in the
' " Odes and Addresses to Great People," John
' Hamilton Reynolds.* On another man of

* ' Few, save perhaps surviving members of the Garrick
' Club, will be found who recollect the name of this writer.
' Yet it was brought before the world by no meaner a judge
' than Lord Byron, who praised his " Safie;" and there is
' hardly an anthology devoted to verse of this century which
' does not include that deliciously musical lyric—

' " Go where the water glideth gently ever,"

' than which our Laureate himself has produced nothing more
' melodious.

' yet greater power and peculiarity, who be-
' longed to the same set, abused as cockney by
' the immaculate Tory critics of Edinburgh, I
' must dwell more in detail : this was George
' Darley, one of the most original human beings
' whom I have ever known, and who cannot
' be forgotten by any of the few who had the
' opportunity, which chance gave me, of study-
' ing so gifted, yet so eccentric, a man near at
' hand.

' Many years ago, when Miss Paton, the
' singer, was in her prime—dividing honours
' as a first-class English singer with Miss
' Stephens—she used to make one of her great
' effects in a ballad " I've been roaming," set to
' ballad music by Horn—one of those delicious
' and refined English tune-composers to whom
' the time present offers no equivalent. The
' words, odd, fantastic, and full of suggestion,
' were by Darley, from a curious pastoral,
' " Sylvia, or the May Queen," a sort of half
' fairy, half-sylvan masque, almost as charming,
' and quite as little intelligible, as a certain
' tale, " Phantasmion," published some years

' ago, and attributed to the gifted Sara Cole-
' ridge, which, possibly, ten persons besides
' myself have read.

  ' At the time when my connection with the
' " Athenæum " began, this strange, reserved
' being, who conceived himself largely shut
' out from companionship with his brother
' poets, by a terrible impediment of speech,
' was wandering in Italy, and sending home to
' the journal in question a series of letters on
' Art, written in a forced and affected style, but
' pregnant with research, unborrowed specu-
' lation, excellent touches by which the nature
' of a work and of its maker are characterised.
' The taste in composition, the general severity
' of the judgments pronounced, might be ques-
' tioned ; but no one could read them without
' being stirred to compare and to think. In
' particular, he laid stress on the elder painters,
' whose day had not yet come for England, on
' Giotto, on Perugino, on Francesco Francia,
' and on Lionardo da Vinci. To myself, as to
' a then untravelled man, the value of these
' letters was great indeed.

'On the return of Darley to London, he
' took up in the " Athenæum " the position of
' dramatic reviewer—not critic to the hour—
' in the most truculent and uncompromising
' fashion conceivable. When Talfourd's " Ion "
' was published, it appeared to myself (as
' it still appears) to be the most noble,
' highly-finished, and picturesque modern
' classical tragedy existing on the English
' stage. It was not its large private dis-
' tribution, not merely the great reputation
' of its author, but the vital, pathetic excel-
' lence of the drama, and the rich poetry of
' the diction, which, on the night of the pro-
' duction of the play at Covent Garden, filled
' that great theatre with an audience the
' like of which, in point of distinction, I have
' never seen in any English theatre. There
' were the flower of our poets, the best of our
' lawyers, artists of every world and every
' quality. There was a poor actor of some
' enterprise and promise, Mr. Cathcart,* who,

* ' He subsequently appeared in London as the " Crom-
' " well " in Miss Mitford's " Charles the First." '

' in the fullness of zeal and expectation, abso-
' lutely walked up to London from Brighton,
' to be present at the first performance.

 ' The success of this was superb, and estab-
' lished its author once for all among the real
' dramatists of England. And yet it was a
' success under disadvantages. With all his
' passion and poetry of execution, and sub-
' tlety of conception, no magic could make
' Mr. Macready thoroughly acceptable as
' the young hero. The part was afterwards
' again and again tried by actresses in
' male attire—always a disappointing, when
' it is not a repulsive, expedient. One could
' not escape from the tones and attitudes
' of Werner, and Virginius, and Macbeth.
' "Ion" has yet to be seen. Nor did the
' charming "Clemanthe" of Miss Ellen Tree
' group well with the hero. The other
' persons of the play were either weakly or
' boisterously presented. There had been
' no particular pains bestowed on scenery or
' appointments. But of the entire, unquestion-
' able triumph of the tragedy, there could not

' be an instant's doubt on the part of any
' unprejudiced spectator. I have rarely been
' so warmed, so moved in any theatre.

'I had met the author at Lady Blessington's;
' and she—in no respect more generously con-
' stant to her friends till the very last than in
' trying to serve younger artists and men of
' letters in whom she fancied promise—pre-
' sented me to the orator and the dramatist of
' that one great play—it may be (for this I
' cannot say), as a writer in connection with a
' rising journal. I have since thought that
' such *must* have been the case, without false
' thought or purpose on her part, but in her
' wish to set me out to the best advantage.
' As matters turned out, her genuine regard
' and desire to present me resulted in no good
' influence on my fortunes, literary or critical,
' but absolutely the reverse.

' An ill chance for me threw the critic's task,
' as regarded the " Athenæum," into the hands
' of Darley—hands never more vigorous than
' when they were using the axe and scalpel.
' That the grace of propriety was utterly want-

‘ ing to him, his own dramas, " Thomas à
‘ " Becket " and " Athelstan " attest.

‘ I was only known to Mr. Talfourd as one
‘ who wrote in the " Athenæum," and having
‘ in person expressed to him what I thought
‘ and felt in regard to the play, it was ne-
‘ cessary for me at once, with the utmost
‘ earnestness, to write to him on the appear-
‘ ance of the criticism against which I had
‘ privately protested, but in vain, with the
‘ strongest possible disclaimer of its unjust
‘ and uncouth severity, and an equally strong
‘ assertion of my own utter powerlessness to
‘ interfere in suppression or mitigation.   My
‘ letter, I fear, was not believed to be sincere.
‘ It was said that, had I been in earnest,
‘ I could easily have attested my sincerity,
‘ by entire withdrawal from a publication so
‘ wicked and malignant—a stringent sugges-
‘ tion,.truly !   But few have admitted the right
‘ of private judgment so grudgingly as the most
‘ advanced Liberals ; few have been so despotic
‘ in their partisanship.   The damage done me
‘ by that article was inconceivable.   Not only

' did it cost me the good understanding of the
' poet himself, but, for years, I was set up as a
' mark to be decried by all the *coterie* round him.
' Whenever I attempted any appearance in
' print, I had such a phrase as this sent to me
' in a newspaper-cutting (lest I should fail to
' see it): the writer· spoke of " the Chorleys and
' " *chawbacons* of literature." Not merely were
' such coarse personalities sent to me, but they
' were righteously forwarded to my family at
' Liverpool, some of whom they succeeded in
' troubling greatly. I can truly say that they
' only disturbed me inasmuch as they placed
' hard material obstacles in the way of my
' maintaining myself as a literary man.

' Some of the specimens of abuse with which
' I was favoured were diverting, rather than
' offensive, by their utter vulgarity. I kept
' by me, for some years, a collection of such
' flowers of rhetoric, the most exquisite of
' which was a letter written in very black
' ink, beginning,

' " You *Worm ! ! !* "

'That this prevailing and explicable anti-
' pathy was a serious injury to me, whenever I
' attempted appearance before the public, is
' beyond doubt. To some degree one may live
' it down; but there are many who to the last
' of an author's career will revert to it, and
' their judgments be influenced accordingly,
' in obedience to the popular adage that
' "where there is smoke, there must be fire."

'I cannot call to mind a writer more
' largely neglected, sneered at, and grudg-
' ingly analysed than myself. I can truly say,
' however, that seriously as this 'most un-
' natural treatment was a hindrance, whether
' to the securing that ease of spirit which
' ought to accompany composition, or in main-
' taining a modest position as regards gain
' without an incessant and anxious struggle,
' I have suffered all my life singularly little
' from bitterness under severe criticism on
' what I have written. I do not remember, in
' this relation between myself and my fellow
' men, to have ever felt resentment, still less a
' desire to retaliate. I deserve no credit for

' this patience or indifference, as may be. It
' was, in great part, a case of temperament; in
' small part, of resolution to go on without
' looking to the right or left, or listening to
' the " black stones" of the Arabian tale,
' which mocked and tried to affright the pil-
' grim as he struggled up the steep hill; nor
' should I have stated the case, save for the
' assistance of those who may come after me.
' Let them count the cost of the struggle
' before they begin ; and once having begun,
' keep their minds as clear as they can of
' comparison and irritation.'

Another illustration of the hatred with
which, even up to a later period, Chorley was
pursued by those who persisted in attributing
to him the censures passed upon themselves
or their friends by the ' Athenæum ' critics,
may be extracted from his journal of August,
1843 :—

'Who would not sicken at times of lite-
' rature, literary men, and literary things when
' such sweetmeats as the following come by
' post—this with a third edition of a Preface to

' " Satan" Montgomery's " Luther," which had
' been sharply handled in the " Athenæum,"
' but had never even been seen by H. F. C. ?—
　' " Be sure your sin will find you out!　One
' " who is well acquainted with Mr. Chorley's
' " infamous trade of defamation and envy
' " against his betters, in the ' Athenæum,'
' " commends the enclosed to his conscience.
' " If not yet too indurated, it will suggest
' " moral justice to a mean and malignant
' " trader in literature!" '
　Happily he now and then received other
testimony of a different quality.　The following letter from G. P. R. James (a novelist
and historian, perhaps, now too little remembered) will be interesting as a disclosure of
the writer's literary aims, and his appreciation
of the service which Chorley was rendering
to his craft :—

" The Cottage, Great Marlow, Bucks,
" 10th October, 1836.

" My dear Sir,

　　" The review of ' The Desultory Man '
in the last ' Athenæum ' is yours.　I recognise

your hand; I recognise your taste and high feeling; and, without wishing you to acknowledge or deny the article, I thank you for it, not because it is laudatory of my book, but because it seizes in a moment, justly and powerfully, one of the greatest objects which I have always had in my literary career, and puts it forth to the public in a way calculated to work a most beneficial change in our literature. That object has been to show that fiction, without being dry and tedious, may be rendered serviceable to every noble principle; may be taught to convey every generous lesson; and, by interesting our good feelings instead of our bad feelings, gain over imagination to the side of virtue, and, without crushing our passions, direct them aright. I thank you most sincerely for having seized and explained my purpose. It was not for me to school my fellow-authors; and, therefore, I have in none of my works put forth either an intimation of my own views or a reproach to others; but you have had an opportunity of reading a lesson, which you have done powerfully as well as gracefully, and I trust, and am sure, you will follow it up by others. Let you and I but labour in this cause, and we will force our brethren of the literary world to follow us. I could not resist my inclination to express these feelings, but will no longer trespass upon your valuable time than to assure you that I am

"Yours most sincerely,

"G. P. R. JAMES." *

A few years later, his favourable review of one of Thackeray's early works—the "Paris Sketch-book"—brought him the following characteristic acknowledgment :—

"13, Great Coram St., Brunswick Sq.,
"18th July, 1840.

"MY DEAR CHORLEY,

"Name anything you wish as a proof of my gratitude, and I will do it for you.

* In another letter of the same year, written to acknowledge Chorley's disavowal of an unfavourable review in the 'Athenæum' of the "History of the Black Prince," Mr. James speaks of the "infinite pleasure" he had derived from the "spirit and style" of Chorley's writings, with which he was too well acquainted to attribute the review in question to their author.

Never was such a good-natured puff as that in the 'Athenæum' of 'Titmarsh.'

"My best respects to Washington.* I called at the Privy Council to see him t'other day; but they told me that Guizot had just stepped out.

"Your faithful and obliged,

"MICHAEL ANGELO T."

A critic might esteem himself fortunate who could establish so good an understanding between himself and the authors he was called upon to dissect. Such tokens of it, however, were as yet quite exceptional in Chorley's experience; nor did he obtain much encouragement from the reception of his early attempts in the reversed position of an author among critics.

He brought up with him to London, in 1834, a volume of sketches and tales, chiefly drawn from observation of Liverpool life, which were published by Mr. Bentley, at

---

* A playful reference to Mr. Henry Reeve, with whom Chorley was then living, and who had just published a translation of M. Guizot's Essay on Washington.

his own risk, in that year, with the author's name, under the title of " Sketches of a Seaport Town."   They were affectionately dedicated, as a first work, to his uncle, Dr. Rutter, whom he calls his " second father."   I do not profess to have given this or any of his earliest productions a careful examination ; but only a cursory reading is required to see that these sketches are very slight in form and substance ; occasionally fanciful, but for the most part flimsily romantic and sensational, indicating no knowledge of the world and merely a superficial study of character.   What is chiefly interesting in them is the testimony they bear to the writer's kindly disposition, his thirsting love for music, his affectionate remembrance of old associations, and the influence which these (more especially the atmosphere of the marvellous, wherein he records himself to have lived,) had wrought upon his mental constitution.   The reference made to Mrs. Hemans, in the sketch entitled " Birds of Passage," is reverential ; and the verses scattered throughout the book are plainly modelled upon her manner. The style, whether of prose or verse, is diffuse, but clear; certain turns of phrase being apparent which were retained almost to the last. Though avowedly drawn from personal observation, these sketches are wholly free from personalities, and were intended, as the preface states, for publication in the place of their composition. The book was kindly noticed by the ' Athenæum,' but met with no more success than so boyish a production deserved.

It was followed, in 1835, by the publication of " Conti, the Discarded; with other Tales and Fancies in Music," for the copyright of which Messrs. Saunders and Otley, on the recommendation of Lady Blessington, gave him £100. The chief tale, " Conti," is a romantic narrative of the fortunes of the unacknowledged son of a wealthy baronet, a musical genius, who, by dint of a persevering application to his art, carves his way to fame and fortune, but becoming entangled in a hopeless passion for a lady of rank, is sacrificed to the exi-

gencies of her caste, and suffers himself to
drift away into temporary ruin and madness.
The preface states that it was long a favourite
fancy of the author's 'to attempt something
' in the style of the German *Kunst-romanen*
' (art-novels), with such modifications as might
' seem called for by the peculiar spirit of our
' national tastes and literature.' This purpose
was reluctantly abandoned, as incompatible
with the scope of fiction, and thus the
" fancies," which were intended to occupy a
larger space in the book, dwindled to a few
leaves; but the original aim was still kept in
view. 'I have long looked,' he says, ' with
' painful interest on the unreckoned-up ac-
' count of misunderstanding and suspicion
' which exist between the world and the artist.
' I have grieved when I have seen the former
' disposed to degrade Art into a mere play-
' thing, to be enjoyed without respect and
' then cast aside, instead of receiving her high
' works as among the most humanising bles-
' sings ever vouchsafed to man by a beneficent
' Creator. I have suffered shame as often

'as I have observed the artist bring his own
'calling into contempt, by coarsely regarding
'it as a mere engine of money-getting, or
'holding it up to reproach by making it the
'excuse for such eccentricities or gross errors
'as separate him from the rest of society.'
The following stories, he proceeds, were
written in the hope of 'awakening some
'sympathy and respect for that art which,
'by a singular anomaly, is held in the lightes
'esteem amongst us, while, at the same time,
'it is more universally preferred than either
'poetry or painting.'

Worthy as was the design, the execution scarcely came up to its height. The
story is too obviously unreal—too little indebted to experience of human nature or
society, to achieve the desired object. Its
merits consist in its occasional fidelity of observation, the portraiture of Silbermann, the
old musician of Nuremberg, being eminently
happy, and its pleasant touches of description,
especially in the scenes of 'Bohemian' life, as
the writer's imagination conceived of it. The

" fancies " of music are mainly extracts from his journals, and display much enthusiasm and some acuteness. The book seems to have failed, in spite of a favourable notice in the ' Athenæum.'

His third work was at once more ambitious and successful, commanding a considerable share of public attention, and attaining to the well-nigh unique distinction (for him) of a second edition. The subject was the life and correspondence of Mrs. Hemans, of whom he had already contributed some personal recollections to the ' Athenæum ' in 1835. After her removal from Liverpool to Dublin, she had addressed several letters to him, which formed the nucleus of the work; but its chief materials were put into his hands by her surviving relatives, and its profits, after his own remuneration had been deducted, were appropriated to the benefit of her children.* The principles that guided him in undertaking her biography are clearly stated in another

* *Vide* a letter to the editor of the ' Athenæum,' August 15, 1839.

letter to his friend at Liverpool, dated July 1835.

"It is more than probable, too (this I mention in confidence), that I may have the arranging and editing of Mrs. Hemans' papers and published works, with the writing of her life. This will be a most laborious undertaking, but for some reasons I should rather like it. She was little understood, even by her friends, and as too blindly admired by some, as she was foolishly and unjustly commented upon by those who would not know her, or could not understand her. Her life was one of misfortune, and false influence on the part of those who had her character in their hands at a time when it might have taken any form; and had they taught her that the imagination gains strength and scope from the reason being cultivated in proportion with it; that nothing is *first rate* and marked for an enduring fame but something which shall profit the world and expand its sympathies, as well as please its ear and its fancy, she might, I know, have taken a stand in our literature far higher than she did. As it was, she was coming to this calmer and loftier state of mind when she died. It is on this principle that I should write the life of any literary person. The responsibilities are too apt to be overlooked by those who associate with and sit in judgment on the gifted; and yet without they are recognised and followed up, I am persuaded no writer will exercise a permanent influence upon the public. We have a proof of this in the cases of Wordsworth and Byron. The former is only coming to his fame; (I mean among the good and worthy); the latter almost lived his out before he died."

Faithful to the canons of biography here laid down, and sympathetic yet discriminating in its estimate of the poetess, this work, published by Messrs. Saunders and Otley, in 1836, under the title of " Memorials of the Life of Mrs. Hemans," constitutes an honourable tribute to her genius, which has not, I believe, been superseded by any more complete memoir.

In America, where her fame was equal to

or higher than that which she enjoyed in her own country, the book was immediately re-published. Its delineation of the influences impressed upon her nature by the scenery and associations amid which she lived, of the tone of culture and refinement diffused by her presence in Liverpool society, and of the calm atmosphere of piety wherein her declining years were passed, is marked by grace and skill. Disclaiming the dignity of a biographer, Chorley wisely confines himself to sketching the mere outline of her life, and expends his labour upon the task of critical analysis, for which he was better fitted. To those who desire a fuller acquaintance with the mind of the poetess than her works supply, these Memorials may be safely commended. If the movement recently set on foot for exalting the intellectual and social *status* of women should ever revolutionise the world, and the historic names which have made the sex illustrious be enshrined in a feminine Walhalla, this biography may yet be destined to attain the distinction it merits.

During 1837 he occupied such hours as he could spare from his regular literary work in the composition of a drama, the subject of which had suggested itself while reading Llorente's "History of the Inquisition." The incident selected was scarcely of sufficient weight to serve as the foundation of a dramatic structure, and required the aid of adventitious materials, which detracted from its importance without having much value of their own. Avowedly written for presentment on the stage, "Fontibel" is pervaded by a general current of action, and interspersed with two or three effective situations, which, if turned to account by intelligent actors, might have procured for it a fair share of success. But its conceptions of character offer no original features, and its language no beauties of thought or fancy that would commend it to the attention of a reader; and as the opportunity of obtaining representation for it was denied him he wisely abstained from giving it publication.

The higher walks of Art, indeed, were as

yet beyond his reach. His critical faculty, wherein his real strength at all times lay, was very early developed; but he arrived late at the full measure of his powers as a creator of character—a measure which, though never attaining to the highest, entitled him, in the judgment of two of his greatest contemporaries, Robert Browning and Charles Dickens, to an honourable place among the dramatists and novelists of the century. Up to this time, however, he had not exceeded mediocrity in the walk of *belles lettres*, to which he chiefly addicted himself. His *vers de société* were often graceful and tuneful, but no more: far inferior to those of his contemporary, Praed; nor even ranking so high in point of finish and skill as the compositions of Fitzgerald and Haynes Bayly, with which they suggest comparison. There are some of his contributions, however, to the ephemeral literature of the boudoir — the " Keepsakes," " Souvenirs," and " Books of Beauty," then in vogue—which display indications of higher quality. The unworldly heart, and genuine simplicity which Chorley retained unspoilt by the frivolity and affectation of the *coteries* wherein this literature was fostered, make themselves felt in such verses. In spite of their incompleteness of construction and frequent poverty of diction, there is often a tender grace about their sentiment, and a quaint flavour about their style, which, to those who knew the writer, are very pleasantly characteristic of him. Of his more strictly lyrical compositions, or songs—of which he wrote a considerable number at this period—it is proper to observe, that they were framed in accordance with a principle laid down by him in a review of Moore's "Irish Melodies" ('Athenæum,' 1834), that the words should never be dissociated in idea from the music, but be regarded as drawings in outline, designed to receive the addition of colour, and incomplete without it, but having none of their own. There is accordingly a thinness of texture, and a bareness of ornament about these lyrics, by which an unprepared reader is likely to be repelled. That they do

not want delicacy of fancy, however, will, I
think, be evident from the following specimens :—

ECHO SONG.

Who calleth where the rock
  The river's haste is staying,
The shepherd's pipe to mock,
Who, with his placid flock
  Strolls on, old tunes a-playing?
      'Tis Echo!
      O merry maiden!
      O thou shy maiden!
      Sing on ever—for ever!

Who in the greenwood dwells,
  Far down its leafy alleys,
And, in faint chime of bells,
The hour of sunset tells
  To the fast glooming valleys?
      'Tis Echo!
      O lonely maiden!
      O thou sad maiden!
      Sing on ever—for ever!

But, strange and wandering sprite!
  Shall never poet see thee?
Shall never stainless knight,
With broadsword keen and bright,
  From thine enchanter free thee?
      No, Echo!

Thou airy maiden!
Thou charmèd maiden!
Viewless ever—for ever!
(CONTI, AND OTHER TALES, vol. iii. p. 130.)

LOVE AT SEA.

Love hath wandered o'er the waves,
　Full of laughter, full of guile;
Now, to sirens in their caves,
　Teaching many a song and wile;
Now, on moon-lit waters calm,
　Rocks the urchin in a shell;
Now, to isles of gold and balm,
Waving with the feathery palm,
　Guides his caravel.
Love hath gone to sea—no more
Let him come on shore.

Love hath flown on noiseless wing,
　Where the ship at anchor lies;
Soon from its unerring string
　Through the sail his arrow flies;
Oft around its slumbering crew
　Pleasant fantasies he weaves,
Dreams of maidens fair and true,
Singing lone the summer through,
　Hid in bowers of leaves.
Love hath gone to sea—no more
Let him come on shore.

Love hath roamed the earth too long,
　With his quiver full of fire;
Ruling all things, weak and strong,
　Sword and sceptre, pen and lyre:

> Fittest is the ocean wild,
>   With its hours of changing tide,
> Empire for the fickle child,
> Now so cunning—now so mild—
>   Now elate with pride.
> Love shall rule the sea :—no more
> Let him come ashore.

(' ATHENÆUM,' 1835.)

Opportunities and means of pursuing that steady course of self-culture essential to the formation of a complete artist were, unfortunately, denied to him at this period of his career. His unremitting labours, both as author and critic, left him comparatively little leisure for the study of works other than those which he was called upon to read or review professionally. Scarcely fewer than a hundred works, good, bad, and indifferent, were annually submitted to his judgment during the early part of his connection with the ' Athenæum.' To a mind, however, so genuinely critical as his, the duty of discrimination is itself a pleasure ; and if his drudgery consisted in meting out justice to inferior literature, he found his relaxation in the quiet perusal of the highest. Of a volume of poems by Wordsworth, published in 1835, he wrote to his friend at Liverpool, in language of the warmest praise — commending it to her study as a "perfect mine of lofty thoughts and beautiful imagery; more refined, and less alloyed by eccentricity, than any of his former works. There are parts of it, which, for the extreme beauty of their thoughts, I could not read to myself without my eyes filling with tears." A few years later, in his journal, he refers to the great enjoyment he had derived from reading the works of Sir Thomas Browne among old authors, and, among modern literature, the recently-published poems of Mr. Tennyson, and the "Rienzi" of Lord Lytton.

His love of pictorial Art—which he was also called upon to study professionally*—was

---

* The principal critiques upon Exhibitions of Works of Art (Royal Academy, British Institution, Water-Colour Society, &c.) that appeared in the 'Athenæum' from 1836 to 1841, and several others of later date, were written by Chorley. So far as I have examined them, they deal only with the poetical element of the subject, and make no pretension to technical connoisseurship.

as genuine as his love of literature, and he lost no opportunity of cultivating his tastes. The exceeding delight with which he had seen the exhibitions of Old Masters at the British Institution and elsewhere, and Sir Thomas Lawrence's collection of their drawings, is more than once recorded in his journal. Under date of August 2nd, 1836, he writes : ' Just returned ' from looking at the Michael Angelo drawings. ' Here again one feels the difference—how ' strongly !—between those who work for im- ' mortality and those who manufacture for the ' hour. I expected anatomical precision and ' grandeur of conception, of course, but hardly ' that I should be able (so little experienced in ' old pictures) to throw myself loose enough of ' the conventionalisms of a taste nourished ' among modern drawing-room works, to be ' able to enjoy and appreciate as much as I ' did. One or two things struck me particu- ' larly. All the Christs have a divinity about ' them I never saw before in any painted idea ' of the Ecce Homo. One in particular, cru- ' cified between the two thieves, though sketchy

' compared with some others, affected me : the
' two outside figures were writhing in the
' agonies of *animal* death ; in Him, the agonies
' of the last hour had no power over the
' patience and sweetness of his nature. The
' head is upturned almost with adoration ; the
' limbs languid and stiffening, but still calm.'
Another entry recounts the equal pleasure he
had derived from a study of the Claude drawings in the same collection, and his fear that
the ' poetical beauty of invention ' displayed
in them was ' one of the lost arts.'

In the drama—apart from its association
with music—he had also a keen enjoyment.
The impersonation of Lear by Forrest, the
American tragedian (at Drury Lane, in
November, 1836), greatly impressed him.
Comparing Forrest with Macready, he says :
' However much Macready moves one at the
' time by the subtle intellect of his personifi-
' cations, I never am much the better for it
' afterwards—never find a word, a look, an
' attitude written on my heart. There are cer-
' tain points of Mr. Forrest's playing that I

'shall never forget to my dying day. . . .
'There is a force, without violence, in his pas-
'sionate parts, which he owes much to his
'physical conformation; but which, thrown
'into the body of an infirm old king (his
'Lear was very kingly), is most awful and
'withering; as, for instance, where he slides
'down upon his knees, with—

> '"For, as I am a man, I think this lady
> '"To be my child, Cordelia."'

Of Talfourd's "Ion," Chorley's opinion
has already been quoted. His estimate of
Lord Lytton's "La Vallière" and its actors
was not so high. He was present at its first
performance, in December, 1836. 'The
'house,' he writes, 'was surly and disposed
'to cavil; the stage management injudicious
'enough to have damned the piece twice over,
'had there not been Miss Faucit in the part of
'the Duchess, a part I should not have fancied
'difficult; and Vandenhoff in Louis Quatorze,
'a dull Brummagem king; and Farren as De
'Lauzun, with the same oily, croaking voice,

' and impotent leer, and sly slope of a step that
' makes his old men pinks of dotage . . . .
' But the play was not damned, thanks to
' Macready's Brageleone.   It will not do, how-
' ever; there are grand things in it, but a want
' of heart palpable to the instinct; and I verily
' think instinct is your best dramatic critic in
' a person of some slight intellect. . The Court
' scenes are flat and flippant, compared with
' what Bulwer might have made them; and
' the verse, though full of imagery and high
' thoughts, by fits which almost rise to the
' unapproachable, so tame and plethoric as to
' be a sensible drawback to the success of the
' piece.'

Lord Lytton's "Lady of Lyons," on the
occasion of its first and very successful representation in February, 1838, was not announced with the author's name, and a good
deal of public curiosity was excited to as-
certain it. 'By some strange blunder,'
as Chorley writes in his journal of the
24th February, ' the "Chronicle" printed my
' name for the author's,' on the day previous.

Congratulatory notes from his friends followed this announcement; which, at first, he did not take the trouble to contradict publicly, 'from a natural imagination that the author and his friends would set it right.' But a day or two later, in answer to a correspondent, 'the "Chronicle" people dis-'tinctly continued to announce the play as 'mine;' and the blunder was repeated by the 'Morning Herald,' in reporting an address of Mr. Macready from the stage, in which, on behalf of the author, he disavowed the "revolutionary tendencies" which some wiseacres had discovered in the design of the play. Upon reading the second announcement in the 'Chronicle,' Chorley at once wrote to disavow the authorship, and the mystery was soon solved by the avowal of the real author. The mistake was a curious one, and not unflattering to so young a writer; testifying, as it did, to his having obtained a recognised position in letters, and a reputation from which far greater achievements were reasonably to be expected. After having seen the play represented, however, he does not appear to have been flattered by the ascription. He thought it 'a sort of cross between 'Kotzebue and Sheridan, with the flat writing 'but human passion of the first in its greater 'scenes, and little brilliant points here and 'there, which remind one of "the blank leaf 'between the Bible and Prayer Book." It is 'as carefully constructed as it is carelessly 'written. For the poetry of the few speeches 'which are in blank verse, there is nothing to 'be said; a snapdragon flame setting up for a 'sunset. In short, as an *opus* it is not much; 'as an acting play it is everything.'

He entertained a much higher opinion of Lord Lytton's powers as a novelist than as a dramatist; and an opportunity of expressing this was afforded him in the course of the same year, when he published "The Authors of England," a series of biographical and critical notices of the most distinguished modern writers, designed to accompany a set of medallion portraits, engraved according to a process recently invented by M. Collas.

The authors thus illustrated were Byron, Coleridge, Lamb, Shelley, Scott, and Mrs. Hemans, among the past, and Bulwer, Campbell, Moore, Southey, Wordsworth, Lady Blessington, Miss Mitford, and Lady Morgan among the living. All these sketches are gracefully and sympathetically written; those on Lord Lytton and Byron being, perhaps, the most discriminating; that on Lamb the most genial in its appreciation. The writer's personal regard is pleasantly, but unobtrusively, shown in the notices of Lady Blessington and Miss Mitford. The book was written by commission for the publisher, Mr. Tilt, who paid him 150*l.* as an *honorarium.* A second edition was called for in 1861.

Articles on literary and musical themes in the 'London and Westminster' and 'British and Foreign' Reviews, and sundry minor sketches occupied his pen during the remainder of 1838. In the following year he completed and published, anonymously, a three-volume novel, entitled "The Lion; a Tale of the Coteries," for the copyright of

which he received 100*l.* from Mr. Colburn.
The theme of this story, like that of " Conti,"
is the career of a " genius " and his relations
with society—a subject that haunted Chorley's
imagination almost to the close of his life, and
of which he has attempted three or four distinct illustrations. The present example differs from the others, in that the career of a
poet instead of a musician is chosen to point
the intended moral. Here again, although
less obviously than was the case in "Conti,"
the execution falls far below the design. The
hero, Robert Brandon, is, after all, but a half-
genius, a youth with imagination enough to
fly and ambition enough to soar, but without
common sense enough to steady his flight, or
industry enough to pursue any quarry at
which he aims. Weak in will, and destitute
of moral principle, he falls an easy prey to the
snares which the lion-hunters of society lay
for his vanity, and the seductions which the
sirens of pleasure offer to his selfishness. A
rustic lad, lowly born and imperfectly educated, he attracts the notice of the magnates

of his village, and renders them a service,
which they repay by obtaining him an honourable appointment in London. Upon the
strength of a meteoric success as a lyrist and
a novelist, and the patronage of a noble family,
he flashes for awhile in the *coteries* of fashionable life; but is speedily eclipsed. by newer
and brighter stars, becomes a *roué* and a
gambler, neglects and breaks the heart of the
gentle girl to whom he was betrothed in the
days of his obscurity, falls madly in love
with his patroness, compromises her reputation, and forfeits her respect; essays dramatic
authorship and hopelessly fails; and, after being
suddenly struck down by an accident which
nearly proves fatal to his shattered constitution, wakes up to a tardy repentance at finding his betrothed dead, his friends beggared,
his patrons estranged, and his fame collapsed.
A hero so shallow-hearted and scatterbrained
can hardly interest any large section of
readers; and as the nominal heroine is almost
a nonentity, pourtrayed so faintly as to be
nearly colourless, the main sources of interest

in a novel of society would seem to be wanting. But though failing in these essential
points, the work is not without power as a
novel of character. The minor personages
are, for the most part, happily individualised;
and the scenes of provincial and metropolitan
life are animated and real. The three Misses
Warble—Miss Christina, jolly, unrefined, and
kindly, with her little vanity about her aristocratic acquaintances, and her little coquetry
about the archdeacon whom she idolises; Miss
Pyarea, with her accomplishment in the art
of cutting paper-likenesses of her favourite
heroes; and Miss Joanna, with her mild
Puritanical proclivities; Sparker, the rich
trader and *parvenu* squire, vulgar, mean,
cowardly, licentious, and Cherry, his coarse,
shrewd, ambitious clerk, are, probably, drawn
from the writer's reminiscences of types familiar to him as a boy. The descriptions of life
in a merchant's office, and of an election scene
in a borough produce the same impression of
having been drawn from personal observation.
The characters and scenery of London society

are scarcely less life-like. Lady Garston, the foolish, unscrupulous caterer for sensation, who values the attractions of a genius and of a millionaire, the eccentricity of a savage and the infamy of a criminal, at an equal rate, as all ministering to the triumph of her skill and the splendour of her *routs*;— Suffield and Almond, the contrasted men of letters, one a superficial and polished worldling, whose pretension and *aplomb* credit him with a reputation that he has never earned; the other, a thoughtful, rough-mannered recluse, whom Fame has passed by, and who chafes under the sense of injustice;—Lord Merivale, the statesman, whose proud reserve conceals his secret ambition, and whose constitutional fear of death haunts him in the very crisis of success;—Lady Merivale, the high-minded, true-hearted wife, proud of the ambition which she has detected and fostered in her husband, yet trembling with anxiety lest the energy she has evoked should be fatal to him;—these and other characters less strongly marked, are obviously portraits at first hand, and not, as was the case with the writer's earlier sketches, derived from recollections of reading, and composed by the aid of fancy. There are occasional scenes—such as the duel after the election—which, if imaginary rather than real, are conceived in a vein of genuine humour. To that which describes the " damnation" of the hero's play, the writer's memory must often afterwards have recurred as painfully prophetic of his own experience. But these merits of directness in observation and truthfulness in delineation are insufficient to redeem the demerits of the book in point of art. The opening chapters especially are pervaded by the sham-romantic, sentimental tone that widely infected English literature at the period when Chorley was writing, and for which his mind had a natural bias, only subdued by the gradual operation of healthier influences, and perhaps never wholly eradicated. This artistic defect, indeed, might of itself have procured the book an ephemeral success, but its faults of design in other and essential features too surely sealed its fate.

' Its failure,' as he notes in his journal, ' was,
' as entire, if not as unexpected, as has attended
' all my former efforts.'   Although he bore up
against depression by habituating his mind
' to expect every drawback and misadventure
' as a matter of course,' he was deeply hurt by
the want of appreciation he experienced in
quarters where he thought himself entitled to
look for it, more especially by ' the wrong-
' headed unfairness' of a review in the ' Athenæum.'   ' It was the rule' with this journal,
however, as he subsequently discovered, and
has noted in one of his autobiographical fragments, ' to avoid the slightest undue favour to
' any of the staff, and even to dismiss the indi-
' vidual publications of contributors, oftentimes
' laconically, sometimes with a searching display
' of errors and weak points, which in more
' flagrant cases might have been passed over.'
That his sensitiveness was due neither to
mortified vanity nor cupidity, but to a natural
craving for sympathy, is, I think, evident from
the humble and almost childlike joy with which
he records in his journal the receipt of a favour-

able review in a magazine so little likely to
influence the reputation or sale of a book as
' Tait's.'   ' The praise,' he says, ' is ample,
' minute, and unmeasured. . . . I dare not
' allow myself to hope that this will have
' any immediate effect in bringing on the
' success which I have sometimes thought the
' Fates obstinately denied me; but it is a satis-
' faction, and one, I think, to be honestly
' enjoyed, to find that one has found an
' answer—the more remote the place, the more
' agreeable.   I do believe my " Lion " to be
' true, and I do think that it ought to find an
' acceptance among the middle classes, as a
' true picture of one section of English life;
' and with this feeling, which I would still
' hope is far behind the inanities of self-com-
' placency, I am thankful that God has per-
' mitted me to receive the strength and
' comfort of perceiving, that what I hope is a
' worthy attempt has been recognised.   Save
' in the mere financial view, I do not care
' much about profit, but it is dreary work to
' write on and on and to make no way; and

' I felt sorely withered this time by the want
' of sympathy under my own roof and in my
' own parish ; and I have been surly, irri-
' table, and distrustful. May it be forgiven
' me ! I am humbled by this unexpected com-
' fort and blessing.'

A notice of his next work, " Music and Manners in France and North Germany," must be preceded by some reference to the tours of 1839, 1840, and 1841, from the memoranda of which it was written. This it will be better to reserve for subsequent chapters.

CHAPTER V.

Personal and social life in London from 1834 to 1841—Shock occasioned by the death of Mr. Benson Rathbone—Influence on his life—Effects of loneliness and ill-health—Counter-influences of personal friendship and love of society—Mr. and Mrs. Procter—Mr. and Mrs. Basil Montagu—Henry Roscoe, Herr Moscheles, Chevalier Neukomm, and N. P. Willis—Lady Blessington and Count D'Orsay—Society at Gore House—*Bon-mots*—La Guiccioli—Interviews with Landor, Isaac Disraeli, and M. Rio—Lord Lytton—Sydney Smith—Miss Mitford and John Kenyon—Wm. Harness—Mrs. Butler and Mrs. Sartoris—George Darley—Justice Talfourd—Mr. Browning—George Grote—Mr. and Mrs. Howitt—Family relations—Deaths of Dr. Rutter and Mrs. Rathbone—Acquaintance with Rogers, Lady Morgan, Miss Landon, and Mrs. Somerville—Visits to Paris—French celebrities—Keeps house with Mr. Henry Reeve — *Réunions*—Lions of London society — Prince Louis Napoleon, &c., &c.

To a nature so affectionate as Chorley's, the separation from his family which his literary life in London involved was of itself a trial, but his loneliness was redoubled by a loss which befell him a few months after his settlement in his new position. His early friend, Mr. Benson Rathbone, met with sudden death by a fall from a stage-coach. The news was conveyed to Chorley just as he was starting to attend a musical festival at Exeter Hall. The shock for a while unmanned him, and "left traces" which he rightly divined were "not to be effaced."

Writing soon afterwards, in · December, 1834, to the same friend in Liverpool to whom he had addressed the letter already quoted, he thus gives his feelings vent :—

"This loss of my dearest and most valued friend has drawn you all closer to me. If I were a person (which, I trust, I am not) generally to forget old affections in new scenes and interests, *he* is not one who could be forgotten; and so hard is it to me to realise his loss, that I am still startling myself by forming plans, &c., with reference to. him, as of old. This is very painful, but it will pass away; and you must know by yourself

how different he was from common friends,
and therefore how much nearer and dearer to
all those whom he *did* love. I am thinking
much of you just now. Anniversaries are
always painful things to me, and I have often
been glad (particularly since I have left home
as a resident) that we were never particular
in keeping them. You will remember me on
Christmas-day, which I believe I shall pass
alone. I am sure that I shall be almost as
much with you as at home; and it will be
a relief I cannot describe when the New Year
is turned. But I trust I can feel that these
painful dispensations do not come altogether
in vain, if they fix our minds more firmly
upon what is true, and just, and excellent in
the midst of the false, hurrying world we live
in. You who dwell quietly among your own
people cannot have the same need of this as
one like myself, living in a whirlpool. . . .

“Your affectionate

“ HENRY F. CHORLEY.”

For years afterwards, the memory of his
lost friend recurred to him in seasons both
of exhilaration and depression, and exercised
an influence over his mind that partook of
a spiritual, almost supramundane, authority.
The impression, of course, became fainter
by the lapse of time, but never wholly faded;
and, as will be subsequently seen, was strong
enough up to the close of his life to consti-
tute the governing motive of his testamentary
dispositions. It was the natural result of his
loneliness, that the tendency to introspection,
to which he was always prone, should be
morbidly aggravated. In default of a living
companion to whom he could communicate
his ambitions and fears, his doubts and sor-
rows, he confided them to his journal, and
dwelt with a scrutiny, often painful in its
minuteness, upon the influences to which his
mind was subjected, and the motives that
actuated his conduct. An echo is wholly
inadequate as a substitute for the human
voice; and a persistent course of self-analysis,
unless steadily counteracted by an equally

persistent association with other minds, is
notoriously prejudicial to mental and moral
health. In Chorley, this habit was intensified
by his physical weakness. From childhood
he was the victim of a chronic affection of the
heart, which eventually proved fatal to him.
Though ordinarily permitting him the free
exercise of his powers, it often incapacitated
him for any exertion, and was seldom long
absent as a source of bodily distress and mental
oppression. It is evident from his journals
that he lived under an abiding sense of the
shadow of impending death; and though
there is no trace of alarm in his references
to the prospect, the tinge of melancholy
imparted to his language betrays the effect
produced by it. To the operation of these
causes may, as I have suggested, be fairly
attributed much of what was peculiar in
his disposition. The habitual nervous sensibility and quaintness of manner, the
too frequent irritability of temper and que-
rulousness of tone that characterised him in
later life were undoubtedly developed, if not

actually generated, by them. That their effect was not even more marked than it was, may be ascribed to the counter-influences of his constitutional youthfulness of spirits and yearning for sympathy. Both of these tendencies in his nature fortunately combined to drive him out of himself, and to moderate, although they failed to overcome, his unhealthy proclivities. When past his sixtieth year, he entered with unflagging enjoyment into social amusements which pall upon most men before thirty; and to the last he preserved a warmth of heart, a readiness of response to offers of friendship from congenial natures, that is usually characteristic only of the young, and with them is ordinarily satisfied by the formation of one or two intimate attachments. In both these respects he seems to me to have been exceptionally gifted. A love of general society and a thirst for personal friendship, were united in him more strongly and less inconsistently than in any other man whom I have known. The fact gives a special character to his reminiscences, which will be sufficiently perceptible as this memoir proceeds.

It was fortunate for him that, possessing these tastes, he was brought into contact, at an early period of his career, with a few distinguished persons who formed the centres of extensive circles. 'By happy chance,' he writes, in a detached passage of his autobiography, 'I had already a few acquaint-
' ances in London, made during previous flying
' visits, whom time converted into friends.
' One or two of these I have the fortune
' to retain yet. A sonnet, which I had written
' in my own copy of " English Songs," gave
' me the pleasure and privilege of knowing
' that delicious lyrist and high-hearted man,
' Barry Cornwall, and through * him the house-
' hold of Mr. and Mrs. Basil Montagu. Both
' were then receiving some of the choicest per-
' sons who have adorned literature and art;
' and the delight and the culture to be gained
' by standing as a background figure in such
' circles cannot be overrated. Well has Miss

---

* An error of memory. *Vide* p. 76.—(H. G. H.)

' Edgeworth remarked in her " Helen," " that
' "there is a time in every man's life when
' " such experiences are of priceless value." ' *

' Before I came to London, too, as a resi-
' dent, another happy chance had introduced
' me into the circle gathered round him by
' Moscheles and his accomplished wife. Since

---

* A pleasant note that Chorley received, two years later, from Mr. Procter, will show the terms on which they stood.

> " 5, Grove-End Place, St. John's Wood,
> " 3rd September, 1836.

" Dear Chorley,

" Pray leave your types, and proofs, and other such matter, and come and dine with us to-morrow at a quarter past five quietly. Walk over in your boots, or hail the omnibus—as you prefer. It is idle to work for posterity always. Give me the despised present. Why should we scorn ourselves for our shadows? Why leave our pudding to be cooked by others, and cater only for fame? Damn fame! What is the good of it? or the pleasure of it? or the use in any way of it? If ever I get any, I'll truckle it away for something solid at the chandler's shop. If you come (and pray do), you will see—besides my wife and myself—a piece of fish, a ditto of meat, and a ditto of pie (or pudding), and the illustrious Cavalier Sigismond Neukomm, who is about to leave this unholy island (on Wednesday), for the sanctities of Paris. The Dilkes I suppose are dead—who are the executors?

> " Yours ever,
> " B. W. Procter."

' the doors of that musical house were closed,
' by the removal of the family to Germany,
' there has been nothing of the kind in this
' city, with the exception of the Kemble house,
' during the short time when Adelaide Kemble
' was on the musical stage.

' A third piece of good fortune for me was
' access to Mr. Henry Roscoe — by far the
' most gifted of the sons of the Italian his-
' torian — who had sufficiently distinguished
' himself at an early age to make his death, ere
' the prime of life and success were entered on,
' a heavy and cruel loss to all who were privi-
' leged to know him.   His accomplishments
' were many and real; his solidity of judg-
' ment was as great as his quickness of sym-
' pathy.   Like all the first-class persons I have
' known, his patience with those inferior to
' himself—patience entirely clear of painful
' condescension — was great and genuine.
' Every one was seen to the best possible
' advantage when beside Henry Roscoe.   He
' could listen and encourage, as well as talk
' with a natural and flowing brilliancy which I

' have never heard exceeded—not three times
' in my life equalled. Though so rich in every
' gift which attracts and retains admiration,
' he was as unhackneyed and as simple in his
' manners as the veriest boy who rattles away,
' out of the fullness of his high spirits, without
' an idea of producing effect. In the hour of
' trouble, he was as tender and patient in sym-
' pathy as a woman—with such instant justice
' and strength of decision as belongs to a
' truthful, acute, and strong man. It was
' impossible to be afraid or affected in his
' company. He was one of those whose early
' departure—whereas so many false and evil
' people are left to cumber and poison the
' earth—tempts those left behind to rebellious
' thoughts and questionings, only to be silenced
' by the solemn words—
' " *What I do thou knowest not now, but thou*
' " *shalt know hereafter.*"
' It has been my duty to lay leaves on many
' tombstones, and, in writing of the deceased, to
' disregard the adage, as false and mischievous
' as any of those which have tended to corrupt

‘ the morals of mankind, “ *De mortuis*,” &c.;
‘ but of none have I been able to speak in
‘ higher and more unqualified terms of admi-
‘ ration than Henry Roscoe.

  ‘ If I have one dying word of counsel for
‘ those entering life when I am leaving it, it
‘ will be,—Live with your superiors—with
‘ those to whom you can look up. There
‘ comes a strength of such a determination
‘ with which “no stranger can intermeddle.” ’

Of the late Herr Moscheles, with whom
Chorley became very intimate, and a less
valuable acquaintance, to whose introduction
this intimacy was due, some further reminiscences are contained in the following
sketch :—

  ‘ Our friendship was cast on in a strange
‘ haphazard fashion. I had written a small
‘ song, which appeared in the “Forget-me-not,”
‘ some forty years ago—the first I ever pub-
‘ lished—and the verses were shown by Mrs.
‘ Bowdich, later Mrs. Lee, who was then
‘ writing her queer Ashantee stories for the
‘ same annual, to the Chevalier Neukomm.

' Of all the men of talent whom I have ever
' known, he was the most deliberate in turning
' to account every gift, every talent, every
' creature-comfort to be procured from others ;
' withal, shrewd, pleasant, universally educated
' beyond the generality of the musical com-
' posers of his period. A man who had been
' largely " knocked about," and had been har-
' dened by the process into the habit or duty
' of knocking about any one whom he could
' fascinate into believing in him. Never was
' any man more adroit in catering for his own
' comforts—in administering vicarious bene-
' volence. Once having gained entrance into
' a house, he remained there, with a possession
' of self-possession the like of which I have
' never seen. There was no possibility of dis-
' lodging him, save at his own deliberate will
' and pleasure. He would have hours and
' usages regulated in conformity with his own
' tastes ; and these were more regulated by in-
' dividual whimsy than universal convenience.
' He must dine at one peculiar hour—at no
' other. Having embraced homœopathy to its

‘ fullest extent, he would have his own dinner
‘ expressly made and provided.   The light
‘ must be regulated to suit his eyes—the tem-
‘ perature to fit his endurance.   But, as rarely
‘ fails to be the case in this world of shy or
‘ sycophantic persons, he compelled obedience
‘ to his decrees; and, on the strength of a
‘ slender musical talent, a smooth diplomatic
‘ manner, and some small insight into other
‘ worlds than his own, he maintained a place,
‘ in its lesser sphere, as astounding and auto-
‘ cratic as that of the great Samuel Johnson,
‘ when he ruled the household of the Thrales
‘ with a rod of iron.   Neukomm had no artistic
‘ vigour or skill to insure a lasting popularity
‘ for his music.   It has passed and gone into
‘ the limbo of oblivion.   Yet, for some five
‘ years, he held a first place in England, and
‘ was in honoured request at every great pro-
‘ vincial music-meeting.   He was at Man-
‘ chester; at Derby, where, I think, his oratorio
‘ “ Mount Sinai ” was produced; most pro-
‘ minent at Birmingham, for which he wrote
‘ his unsuccessful “ David”—for a while called

' " The King of Birmingham." I question
' whether a note of his music lives in any
' man's recollection, unless it be " The Sea,"
' to the spirited and stirring words of Barry
' Cornwall.

' This song made at once a striking mark
' on the public ear and heart. The spirited
' setting bore out the spirited words; and
' the spirited singing and saying of both by
' Mr. Henry Phillips had no small share in
' the brilliant success. I can only call to mind
' another modern sea song—Bishop's " O Firm
' as Oak," which in the least holds its place by
' the side of Neukomm's in right of merit.
' Neither are sung for the moment. Both may
' return. The Chevalier was as cunning in his
' generation as his poet was the reverse. On
' the strength of this success and his partner's
' simplicity, the musician beguiled the poet to
' write some half-hundred lyrics for music, the
' larger number of which are already among
' the classics of English song, in grace and
' melody recalling the best of our old drama-
' tists, and surprisingly little touched by con-

‘ ceit.   Will it be believed, that for such ad-
‘ mirable service the noble-hearted poet was
‘ never even offered the slightest share in gains,
‘ which would have had no existence save for
‘ his suggesting genius, by the miserable Che-
‘ valier ? It only dawned on him that his share
‘ of the songs must have some value, when the
‘ publishers, without hint or solicitation, in
‘ acknowledgment of the success, sent a slight
‘ present of jewellery to a member of his
‘ family.   It is sadly true that too many mu-
‘ sicians have shown a like disregard of the
‘ laws of *meum* and *tuum* in regard to the
‘ verse they have set.   The case, in every one’s
‘ interest, cannot be too plainly stated ; but a
‘ more flagrant illustration does not exist than
‘ the dealings of Neukomm with the author of
‘ “ Mirandola.”

‘ Enough of a distasteful subject.   My own
‘ gains from the notice of the Chevalier were of
‘ a different quality—gains beyond the desert
‘ of an obscure rhymester trying to struggle
‘ into print.   It was on one of those hurried
‘ visits to London, without the excitement of

' which, the hated drudgery of mercantile life
' among uncongenial spirits would have be-
' come intolerable, that M. Neukomm intro-
' duced me to one of the happiest musical
' households and family circles I have ever
' known—that of Moscheles. This was only
' a few years after his marriage. Our good
' understanding remained unbroken till the
' last hour of his life. All that he had of
' what was genial in his nature, and agreeable
' in his life I was permitted to enjoy. In his
' house were to be met the best celebrities of
' literature and art. The standard of general
' cultivation, morals, and manners among mu-
' sicians has risen largely during the last five-
' and-thirty years; but there has been, I re-
' peat, no ground such as that house offered,
' where the best of the best and the newest
' of the new met on such perfect terms of ease
' and equality. I have good reason to speak
' of it with most grateful remembrance.

' I have never known a man in whom
' two entirely distinct natures—those of ex-
' cessive caution and equal liberality—were so

' intimately combined. The caution in money
' matters, the liberality in time, counsel, in-
' terest given without stint or envy to all
' contemporary or rising artists. I detected
' no trace of jealousy in his nature ; on the
' other hand, a curiosity to make acquaintance
' with all that was new or promising, and
' as much liberality of judgment as was con-
' sistent with a closeness of character, which
' intensified his nationality.'

Another acquaintance, not more permanent
or valuable in himself than the Chevalier
Neukomm, but through whom Chorley obtained a valued and lifelong friend, was the
late N. P. Willis. They met, as the following
notice tells us, by an accident :—

' In the autumn of 1834, while travelling
' in Italy, Mr. N. P. Willis had met with a
' gentleman well acquainted with my elder
' brother. This gentleman had given a letter
' for my brother to Mr. Willis, who gathered
' introductions to persons of every degree of
' fortune or of every circle more solicitously
' than any one whom I have ever seen. Mr.

' Willis, meeting me by chance at a friend's
' house, naturally enough mistook me for the
' person to whom Mr. ——'s letter was ad-
' dressed, and I was as naturally glad to make
' an agreeable acquaintance. And agreeable
' I found Mr. Willis, and kindly in his way,
' though flimsy in his acquirements and flashy
' in his manners—a thorough literary getter-
' on, but a better-natured one than many I
' have since known. At that time of my life,
' it seemed a necessity for me to have some one
' to talk over my schemes with, and to show
' my attempts to. He, too, seemed to have the
' same fancy, though it was an unequal bar-
' gain, since he wrote much less, because far
' more carefully than I. In short, it was an
' intimacy that could not, under any circum-
' stances, have lasted long, but which, while
' it did last, was pleasant to both.'

A retrospective journal of 1837 describes
somewhat more minutely the impression
which this once celebrated *littérateur* made
upon Chorley at the first blush :

' There was something very agreeable and

‘ fascinating in his manner—a sort of gentle
‘ flattery that made you feel as if he had be-
‘ come peculiarly interested in you. I have
‘ been always too prone to attach myself to any
‘ one who would let me, so took him up at once
‘ on his own showing. Then he was a lite-
‘ rary man of my own age, and about my own
‘ means, with as much less of thought as he
‘ had more of cleverness. And I believe, for
‘ a time, he did like me in his way ; gave me
‘ good advice about dress, manners, &c.—a
‘ little too magnificently I *now* think—and cer-
‘ tainly was of use to me in making me mo-
‘ dulate my voice. We passed a part of every
‘ day together ; dreamed dreams, and schemed
‘ schemes, and canvassed our tailors’ bills, &c.
‘ He read to me his ‘ Melanie ’ in progress,
‘ and, which was better, listened while I read
‘ to him. . . . With great diffidence I sent
‘ through him a *chanson* to my Lady Blessing-
‘ ton, who was then his great patroness and
‘ friend ; and this he gave her with many kind
‘ words. It was “ Love at Sea ;” on which
‘ she expressed a wish to see me.’

Chorley's acquaintance with Willis appears to have closed with the latter's departure 'for ' Scotland, full of the intention (as he pro- ' fessed himself) of marrying a Scotch lady ' with red hair, who (according to his usual ' story) had fallen in love with him. But he ' had fancied that Lady Blessington had ' already been smitten! As he had a box full ' of locks of hair, trophies of his continental ' Don Giovannism, perhaps he was excus- ' able.'

Before he left town, however, he lastingly befriended Chorley by the introduction to Lady Blessington above referred to. Of this brilliant woman, and the accomplished man with whom her name will always be asso- ciated, we have the following reminis- cence :—

' Lady Blessington was then gathering ' about her a circle of the younger literary men ' of London, in addition to the older and more ' distinguished friends made by her before her ' widowhood. I went with Willis to the studio ' of Mr. Rothwell, who was engaged on a half-

‘ length portrait of her, which he never, I
‘ believe, completed, and was introduced to
‘ her. She said a few kind words in that win-
‘ ning and gracious manner which no woman’s
‘ welcome can have ever surpassed ; and from
‘ that moment till the day of her death in
‘ Paris, I experienced only a long course of
‘ kind constructions and good offices. She was
‘ a steady friend, through good report and evil
‘ report, for those to whom she professed friend-
‘ ship. Such faults as she had belonged to her
‘ position, to her past history, and to the dis-
‘ loyalty of many who paid court to her by
‘ paying court to her faults, and who then
‘ carried into the outer world depreciating re-
‘ ports of the wit, the banter, the sarcasm,
‘ and the epigram, which but for their urgings
‘ and incitements would have been always
‘ kindly, however mirthful.

‘ She must have had originally the most
‘ sunny of sunny natures. As it was, I have
‘ never seen anything like her vivacity and
‘ sweet cheerfulness during the early years
‘ when I knew her. She had a singular power

' of entertaining herself by her own stories;
' the keenness of an Irishwoman in relishing
' fun and repartee, strange turns of language,
' and bright touches of character. A fairer,
' kinder, more universal recipient of every-
' thing that came within the possibilities of her
' mind, I have never known. I think the only
' genuine author whose merits she was averse
' to admit was Hood; and yet she knew Ra-
' belais, and delighted in " Elia." It was her
' real disposition to dwell on beauties rather
' than faults. Critical she could be, and as judi-
' ciously critical as any woman I have ever
' known, but she never seemed to be so wil-
' lingly. When a poem was read to her, or a
' book given to her, she could always touch on
' the best passage, the bright point; and rarely
' missed the purpose of the work, if purpose it
' had. When I think of the myriads I have
' known who, on such occasions, betwixt a
' desire to show sagacity, slowness to appre-
' ciate, or want of tact in expression, flounder
' on betwixt commonplace which is not compli-
' mentary, and disquisitions that are rather

' hard to bear, I return to her powers and
' ways of accepting as among the lost graces,
' which have been replaced (say the optimists)
' by something truer and more solid. I doubt it.

' Her taste in everything was towards the
' gay, the superb, the luxurious; but, on the
' whole, excellently good. Her eye was as
' quick as lightning; her resources were many
' and original. It will not be forgotten how,
' twenty years ago, she astounded the Opera-
' goers by appearing in her box with a plain
' transparent cap, which the world in its ignor-
' ance, called a Quaker's cap; and the best of all
' likenesses of her, in date later than the lovely
' Lawrence portrait, is that drawing by Chalon
' in which this " tire " is represented, with some
' additional loops of ribbon. So, too, her houses
' in Seamore Place and at Kensington Gore
' were full of fancies which have since passed
' into fashions, and which seemed all to belong
' and to agree with herself. Had she been
' the selfish Sybaritic woman whom many who
' hated her, without knowing her, delighted to
' represent her, she might have indulged these

' joyous and costly humours with impunity; but
' she was affectionately, inconsiderately liberal
' —liberal to those of her own flesh and blood
' who had misrepresented and maligned her,
' and who grasped at whatever of bounty she
' yielded them, with scarcely a show of cor-
' diality in return, and who spread the old,
' envious, depreciating tales before the service
' had well been done an hour!

' What her early life had been, I cannot
' pretend to say. I have heard her speak of
' it herself once or twice, when moved by very
' great emotion or injustice from without. And
' what woman, in speaking of past error, is
' unable to represent herself as more sinned
' against than sinning? I have heard, on the
' other hand, some who professed an intimate
' knowledge of her private concerns and past
' adventures (which profession is often more
' common than correct), attack her with a bit-
' terness which left her no excuse, no virtue, no
' single redeeming quality—representing her as
' a cold-blooded and unscrupulous adventuress,
' only fit to figure in some novel by a Defoe,

' which women are not to read. That this
' cannot have been true, every friend of hers
' will bear me out in asserting—and she kept
' her friends. The courage with which she
' clung to her attachments long after they
' brought her only shame and sorrow, spoke
' for the affectionate heart, which no luxury
' could spoil and no vicissitude sour.'

' The wit of Count d'Orsay was more
' quaint than anything I have heard from
' Frenchmen (there are touches of like quality
' in Rabelais)—more airy than the brightest
' London wit of my time, those of Sydney Smith
' and Mr. Fonblanque not excepted. It was
' an artist's wit, capable of touching off a cha-
' racter by one trait told in a few odd words.
' The best examples of such *esprit* when written
' down, look pale and mechanical : something
' of the *aroma* dies on the lips of the speaker ;
' but an anecdote or two may be tried, bringing
' up as they do the magnificent presence, and
' joyous, prosperous voice and charming tem-
' per of him to whom they belong.

' When Sir Henry Bulwer was sent on a
' diplomatic mission to Constantinople, " *Quelle*
' " *bétise*," was the Count's exclamation, " to
' " send him there among those Turks, with
' " their beards and their shawls—those big,
' " handsome fellows—a little grey man like
' " that! They might as well have sent one
' " whitebait down the Dardanelles to give
' " the Turks an idea of English fish."

' I have heard the Count tell, how, when
' he was in England for the first time (very
' young, very handsome, and not abashed), he
' was placed at some dinner-party next the late
' Lady Holland. That singular woman, who
' adroitly succeeded in ruling and retaining a
' distinguished circle, longer than either fasci-
' nation or tyranny might singly have accom-
' plished, chanced that day to be in one of her
' imperious humours. She dropped her nap-
' kin; the Count picked it up gallantly; then
' her fan, then her fork, then her spoon, then
' her glass; and as often her neighbour stooped
' and restored the lost article. At last, how-
' ever, the patience of the youth gave way,

' and on her dropping her napkin again, he
' turned and called one of the footmen behind
' him. "Put my *couvert* on the floor," said he.
' " I will finish my dinner there; it will be
' " so much more convenient to my Lady
' " Holland."
 'There was every conceivable and incon-
' ceivable story current in London of the extra-
' vagance of the "King of the French" (as the
' Count d'Orsay was called among the sporting
' folk in the Vale of Aylesbury); but it was
' never told that he had been cradled, as it
' were, in an ignorance of the value of money,
' such as those will not believe possible who
' have been less indulged and less spoiled, and
' who have been less pleasant to indulge and to
' spoil than he was.   But extravagance is like
' collection as a passion.   Once let it be owned
' to exist, and there will be found people to
' forgive it, and to feed it, and to find it with
' new objects.   When an American gentleman,
' the gifted Mr. Charles Sumner, was in Eng-
' land, his popularity in society became, justly,
' so great and so general, that his friends began

' to devise what circle there was to show him
' which he had not yet seen, what great house
' that he had not yet visited. And so it was
' with Count d'Orsay. His grandmother, Ma-
' dame Crawford, delighted in his beauty, and
' his sauciness, and his magnificent tastes.
' When he joined his regiment, she fitted
' him out with a service of plate, which made
' the boy the laughingstock of his comrades.
' Whether it was broken up into bits, or played
' for at *lansquenet*, or sunk in a marsh, I cannot
' recollect; but one or other catastrophe hap-
' pened, I do know. He was spoiled during
' most of his life by every one whom he came
' near; and to one like myself, endowed with
' many luxurious tastes, but whom the disci-
' pline of poverty had compelled prematurely
' to weigh and to count, it was a curious sight
' to see, as I often did in the early days of our
' acquaintance, how he seemed to take it for
' granted that everybody had any conceivable
' quantity of five-pound notes. To this fancy
' the Lichfield, Beaufort, Chesterfield, Massey
' Stanley set, among whom he was conversant,

' ministered largely. He spent their money
' for them royally, and made them fancy they
' were inventing all manner of sumptuous
' and original ways of spending it. When the
' crash and the downfall came, and the Count
' owned himself beaten, ruined, "done for at
' " last" (as the familiar phrase runs), he said,
' " Well, at least, if I have nothing else, I will
' " have the best umbrella that ever was."
' The wish was granted by a lady, who brought
' the immured man of pleasure in difficulties an
' umbrella from Paris, with a handle set in
' jewels. That was a type of Count d'Orsay's
' ideas of poverty and bad weather, and re-
' trenchment!

' But never was Sybarite so little selfish
' as he. He loved extravagance—waste, even.
' He would give half a sovereign to a box-
' keeper at a theatre as a matter of course, and
' not ostentation; but he could also bestow time,
' pains, money, and recollection, with a muni-
' ficence and a delicacy such as showed what
' a real princely stuff there was in the nature
' of the man whom Fortune had so cruelly

' spoiled. He had " the memory of the heart "
' in perfection.'

The thoughtful kindness shown by Lady Blessington, as the presiding genius in an extensive sphere of literary and social notabilities, to a young and untried man of letters such as Chorley, at the outset of his career, was of the utmost value to him, and merited the grateful acknowledgment it received. She seems to have conceived a genuine regard for him, and taken an active interest in his concerns; inviting him habitually to her dinners and *soirées*, enlisting him as a contributor to the Annuals of which she was editress, and giving the weight of her personal recommendation to the publishers with whom he wished to negotiate. The homage which was all that he had to offer in return, was loyally rendered, as many a generous review and flattering verse may attest. The good understanding between them was uninterrupted. Of the gloom by which her closing days were clouded he was no unmoved spectator; and her death, in 1850, is chronicled in his journal as the rupture of one of his cherished ties. In such of her letters as he has preserved there are no marked traces of the writer's individuality; but one may be inserted as somewhat less colourless than the rest, and evidence of the kindly relations subsisting between the correspondents :

"Gore House, May 20th, 1844.

" My dear Mr. Chorley,

" Will you have the kindness to forward the accompanying note to your brother? I am greatly pleased with the sonnets. What a charming and graceful manner of commemorating his tour! The volume is really too good not to be published, for it would do the author credit.*   A thousand thanks for all your kind offers for my Annuals. What will you say when I tell you that I have not yet seen a single plate or drawing for the ' Keepsake ?' You will be glad to hear that the Cte. Auguste de Gramont is to be married to Mademoiselle de

---

* A series of poems, by the late John Rutter Chorley, is apparently the subject of this reference.

Segur on the 5th of June. The lady is beautiful enough to justify a *mariage d'amour,* which this one is, and rich enough to satisfy a *mariage de raison.* A great family, and, in short, in every point an admirable alliance. I read with great delight, on Saturday, the admirable letter on Lord Byron's poetry, and honour the writer, whoever he may be. I regret the engagements which prevent our seeing you as often as we could wish; but we are not summer friends, so that I hope, when winter comes, we shall enjoy more of your society. Say all that is most kind for me to your sister, and believe me always,

" Your sincere friend,

" M. BLESSINGTON."

At Lady Blessington's residence in Seamore Place, and subsequently at Gore House, he was, as I have said, a frequent and welcome guest. Of the constantly changing and distinguished circle which the charm of her grace and wit attracted round her, he appears to have been an unobtrusive, but a

shrewdly observant member. Many a *bon-mot*
and characteristic anecdote, which first obtained currency in these *salons*, some of which
have passed from the world's memory, and
may be worth recalling, are registered in his
journal.   Here, for example, are two stories of
Theodore Hook, which to many ears will be
as good as new :

'*Aug.* 15*th*, 1835.—Last night, Westma-
' cott told a *Hookism* at Lady Blessington's
' worthy of being kept.   He was at some large
' party or other where the lady of the house
' was more than usually coarsely anxious to get
' him to make sport for her guests. A ring
' formed round him of people only wanting a
' word's encouragement to burst out into a vio-
' lent laugh. "Do, Mr. Hook; *do* favour us !"
' said the lady for the hundredth time. "In-
' " deed, madam, I can't; I can't, indeed. I am
' " like that little bird, the canary ; can't lay
' " my eggs when any one is looking at me."'

'*Aug.* 18*th*, 1838.—I must post one anec-
' dote of Theodore Hook. . . . He was dining
' at Powell's the other day, to meet Lord Can-

‘ terbury, and the talk fell upon *feu* Jack
‘ Reeve. . . . “ Yes,” said Theodore, when
‘ they were speaking of his funeral, “ I was
‘ “ out that day : *I met him in his private box,*
‘ “ *going to the pit !*” ’

Here again is a specimen of Fonblanque’s
biting humour. When Dickens mentioned
his intention of visiting America —‘ Why,’
was the retort, ‘ aren’t there disagreeable
‘ people enough to describe in Blackburn or
‘ Leeds ?’

The following is of anonymous authorship.
When one Mr. Sparks was appointed to a
bishopric, a rival candidate consoled himself
with the reflection—‘ Man is born to trouble
‘ as the sparks fly upward !’

The following anecdote of Byron, told on
the authority of his travelling companion,
Mr. Trelawney, a frequent visitor at Gore
House, is eminently characteristic. When
Byron, Shelley, and Trelawney were in Italy
together, ‘ some small secret (perhaps a bit of
‘ London scandal) had come over in an English
‘ letter, of which Shelley and Trelawney were

' the sole possessors. He (Byron) was most
' eager to discover this, and, when riding out
' with the latter, went to the childish length of
' jumping off his horse, declaring that he would
' kneel down in the middle of the road and
' never rise—that he would lie down and rot—
' and let his companion ride over him, &c., &c.,
' if he was not satisfied. On which, Trelawney
'.improvised some *historiette* or other, so that
' Lord Byron got up again contented. A few
' minutes afterwards, La Guiccioli's carriage
' appeared in sight.   Lord Byron rode up to it,
' brimful of his secret, which he presently dis-
' charged upon his *donna*. When he rejoined
' his companion, Trelawney upbraided him
' with treachery. "Damn it! what's a secret
' " good for else? Do you think I would
' " have done as I did if I had not meant to
' " tell it?" His chagrin and humiliation
' may be imagined on being made acquainted
' with the real state of the case.'

The lady to whom reference is made in this
anecdote was also a visitor at Gore House.
Chorley met her there more than once, and

afterwards renewed the acquaintance in Paris. He describes her, after their first meeting, in September, 1835, as ' precisely what I had ' expected to find her. Sweet, artless, earnest, ' untidy, very guiltless of mind, with a pearly ' white complexion, a huge foot, and profuse ' hair—the colour of a pale ripe nut—with all ' the gesticulation and *abandon* of an Italian ' woman, and something high-bred in spite ' of all.'

Landor, Isaac Disraeli, Fonblanque, and Lord Lytton (then Mr. Bulwer) were among the most remarkable persons whom he was in the habit of meeting in this circle. Of Landor he saw a good deal, and records several noteworthy traits. The first impression produced by him was that of ' a positive, demon- ' strative man, full of prejudice, with a head ' reminding me of Hogarth's, with his dog at ' his side.' Two or three sketches of him in society, as contrasted with opposing tempera- ments, bring out forcibly the leading lines of his character :

' *May 8th*, 1838.—Yesterday evening, I had

' a very rare treat—a dinner at Kensington
' *tête-à-tête* with Lady Blessington and Mr.
' Landor; she talking her best, brilliant and
' kindly, and without that touch of self-con-
' sciousness which she sometimes displays
' when worked up to it by flatterers and
' gay companions. Landor, as usual, the very
' finest man's head I have ever seen, and
' with all his Johnsonian disposition to tyran-
' nise and lay down the law in his talk, re-
' strained and refined by an old-world courtesy
' and deference towards his bright hostess, for
' which *chivalry* is the only right word. There
' was never any one less of "a pretty man;" but
' his tale of having gone from Bristol to Bath,
' to find a moss-rose for a girl who had desired
' one (I suppose for some ball), was all natural
' and graceful, and charming enough. . . .
' Well, this, with a thousand other delightful
' things which there is no remembering, went
' by, when Mr. Disraeli the elder was an-
' nounced. I had never seen him before;
' and, as of course they talked and I heard,
' I had the luxury of undisturbed leisure

' wherein to use eyes and ears. An old
' gentleman, *strictly*, in his appearance ; a
' countenance which at first glance (owing,
' perhaps, to the mouth, which hangs) I fancied
' slightly chargeable with stolidity of expres-
' sion, but which developed strong sense as it
' talked ; a rather *soigné* style of dress for so
' old a man, and a manner good-humoured,
' complimentary (to Gebir), discursive and
' prosy, bespeaking that engrossment and in-
' terest in his own pursuits which might be
' expected to be found in a person so patient
' in research and collection. But there is a
' tone of the *philosophe* (or I fancied it), which
' I did not quite like; and that tone (addressing
' the instinct rather than the judgment) which
' is felt or imagined to bespeak (how shall it
' be ?) absence of high principle. No one can
' be more hardy in his negation than Mr. Fon-
' blanque ; in no one a sneer be more triumph-
' antly incarnate—and it is sometimes very
' withering and painful ; but he gives you
' the impression of considering destruction and
' denial to be his mission ; whereas there is an

' easy optimism and expediency associated
' with my idea of Mr. Disraeli, which, while it
' makes his opinions less salient, increases their
' offence. This is very hardy in the way of
' generalisation! I did not like the manner,
' above all things, in which he talked about
' the Slave Trade and Wilberforce's life—how
' the latter was set down as a mere *canter*.
' (Curious to hear this by his own fireside!)
' Then he advanced a theory about Shake-
' speare's having been long in exciting the
' notice he deserved, as compared with Ben
' Jonson and other dramatists, which was
' either incompletely stated, or based on shal-
' low premises—most probably the former. It
' gave occasion to a very fine thing by Lan-
' dor: " Yes, Mr. Disraeli, the oak and the
' " ebony take a long time to grow up and
' " make wood, but they last for ever!" '

As a final sketch, may be quoted a scene
at which Landor was contrasted with M. Rio.
This gentleman, the author of "Art Chrétien,"
Chorley describes as ' one of the most pic-
' turesque-looking men ' he had seen, and the

first he had encountered 'of the honest and
' picturesque romanticists of the Middle Ages.
' An enthusiast, but without that distressing
' measure of enthusiasm behind which I at
' least linger, and in proportion to the heat
' of which my mind, whether out of conceit
' or want of sincerity I know not, grows
' cold.' On the occasion referred to, Landor
was 'more petulant and paradoxical than
' I ever heard him, saying violent and odd
' rather than the clever and poetical things
' he is used to say ; of all things in the world,
' choosing to attack the Psalms. M. Rio, who
' is an Ultramontane Catholic, winced under
' this, as any man of good taste must have
' done. Lady Blessington put a stop, how-
' ever, to this very displeasing talk by saying,
' in her arch, inimitable way, "*Do* write some-
' " thing better, Mr. Landor ! " '

With Lord Lytton, Chorley was frequently
brought into contact, and had better opportunities of judging his character than mere drawing room intercourse can afford. The impression produced was not very favourable. In

an entry of Oct. 31st, 1836, Chorley writes :
' We walked home together (from Lady Bles-
' sington's), and in his cloak and in the dusk
' he unfolded more of himself to me than
' I had yet seen; though I may say that I
' had guessed pretty much of what I did see—
' an egotism—a vanity—*all* thrown up to the
' surface. Yes, he is a thoroughly *satin* cha-
' racter; but then it is the *richest* satin.
' Whether it will wear as well as other less
' glossy materials remains to be seen. There
' was something inconceivably strange to me
' in his dwelling, with a sort of hankering,
' upon the Count d'Orsay's physical advan-
' tages; something beneath the dignity of an
' author, my fastidiousness fancied, in the
' manner in which he spoke of his own works,
' saying that the new ones only interested
' him as far as they were *experiments*. It is
' a fine, energetic, inquisitive, romantic mind,
' if I mistake not, that has been blighted
' and opened too soon. There wants the
' repose, "the peace that passeth all under-
' " standing," which I must believe (and if it

' be a delusion, I hope I shall never cease to
' believe) is the accompaniment of the *highest*
' mind.'

A little later, after a *tête-à-tête* dinner with
Bulwer at the Reform Club, Chorley writes :
'I found all my judgments confirmed by fur-
' ther experience, both as to cleverness and
' self-conceit. I am not quite sure about the
' *heart*, or its opposite; but it is infinitely
' amusing to discover what there is no escaping
' from, that he makes personal appearance his
' idol, and values Voltaire as much on being a
' tall man as on his satires or essays, &c. It is
' unlucky to make so many *valets de chambre*
' of all one's acquaintances, when a little re-
' serve and calmness of mind might make a
' tolerable hero of a man.'

The differing estimates which he entertained of Lord Lytton's powers as a novelist,
and as a dramatist, have been adverted to elsewhere. At one of these expressions of critical
independence the author seems to have taken
umbrage, and a stop was thus put to an acquaintance which did not promise to be pros-

perous. In later life, however, the breach appears to have been healed, as I infer from two or three friendly notes, including an invitation to Knebworth, addressed to him by Lord Lytton, which Chorley has preserved among his correspondence.

The familiarity which he attained with the habits of the social circle of which Lady Blessington was the leader, brought about, in a way that was creditable to both the parties concerned, his acquaintance with one who was among the chief ornaments of the rival circle presided over by Lady Holland; perhaps the greatest wit of modern times—Sydney Smith. Of this acquaintance Chorley has left a brief reminiscence. He describes him as ' the ' only wit, perhaps, on record, whom brilliant ' social success had done nothing to spoil or ' harden; a man who heartened himself up to ' enjoy, and to make others enjoy, by the sound ' of his own genial laugh; whose tongue was ' as keen as a Damascus blade when he had to ' deal with bigotry, or falsehood, or affectation; ' but whose forbearance and gentleness to those,

‘ however obscure, whom he deemed honest,
‘ were as healing as his sarcasm could be
‘ vitriolic. Of all that passed under Lady
‘ Blessington's roof, the wildest stories were
‘ current in the outer world, among women of
‘ genius especially, who hated with a quint-
‘ essence of feminine bitterness, a woman able
‘ to turn to account, so brilliantly as Lady Bles-
‘ sington did, the difficulties of her position, in-
‘ evitable because referable to the events of her
‘ early life. Lady Holland—who ruled her sub-
‘ jects with a rod of iron, and who, supported
‘ by her lord's urbanity, his literary distinction
‘ and political influence, ventured on an amount
‘ of capricious insolence to the obscure, such as
‘ counterbalanced the recorded deeds of muni-
‘ ficence by which her name was known abroad
‘ and at home—had not a more distinguished
‘ court of men around her than Lady Blessing-
‘ ton assembled. It was a duel betwixt gall at
‘ Kensington and wormwood at Gore House.
‘ Sydney Smith was one of Lady Holland's
‘ “ court-cards,” and was, naturally enough,
‘ prepared to receive her tales of what passed

' in the smaller but livelier Kensington house-
' hold. On one occasion, at the house of a
' third person, I heard him, primed with her
' slander, speak of the high gambling by which
' Lady Blessington, at the instance of d'Orsay,
' lured foolish youths of cash and of quality to
' Gore House.   The fact was, there never was
' such a thing there as play, or the shadow of
' play—not even a rubber of whist.   I stayed
' in the house—I was there habitually and per-
' petually during many years, early and late,
' and as habitually and perpetually was driven
' to my own lodging, at midnight, by Count
' d'Orsay, who had a schoolboy's delight in
' breaking the regulations of St. James's Park,
' which then excluded every one save royal
' personages from passing after midnight. After
' this, he would go to Crockford's, and play;
' but with these matters Lady Blessington had
' nothing to do, beyond the original mistake
' of harbouring so exhausting an inmate as he
' was.   This is a digression necessary to that
' which is to follow. When I heard the scandal
' retailed as above by Sydney Smith—told as a

'fact by such a just and good man, and yet
'with a condiment of such mirth as makes
'scandal sweeter—I felt that I must speak out.
'It was cruelly hard to do so, but I did get out
'the real version of the story. "Thank you,"
'said the old wit to the obscure penny-a-liner;
'"thank you for setting me right." And
'from that time till the day of his death his
'kindness to me was unbroken.

'Before his death he called in his letters,
'with a view to their destruction; averse to the
'misuse which could be made, according to the
'flagrant fashion of our time, of every scrap
'of written paper, by the literary ghouls who
'fatten their purses in the guise of biographers.
'Before one series of such intimate and lively
'communications was delivered up to him, an
'intimate and a prized friend, to whom they
'were addressed, asked him whether he had
'any objection to my reading them. "No,"
'was the answer; "he is a gentleman." The
'sanction gives a relish beyond all price to my
'recollection of the exquisite whimsies, the
'keen appreciation of character, and the jus-

' tice in judgment which these letters con-
' tained.'*

Another early-formed and long-enduring intimacy of Chorley's was made with Miss Mitford. 'It is long,' he writes, in his journal of May, 1836, soon after their first acquaintance, ' since I have been so pleased ' with any one, whether for sweetness of voice, ' kindness and cheerfulness of countenance ' (with *one* look which reminds me of a look I ' shall meet no more), or high-bred plainness ' of manner. I was fascinated.' Their friendship was cemented by two or three visits which he paid to her cottage at Three Mile Cross, and by frequent correspondence. Miss

---

* In a letter of March, 1845, to his friend in Liverpool, Chorley thus refers to the death of Sydney Smith:—" I have been deeply concerned by the loss of my kind and indulgent friend, Mr. Sydney Smith. To us it makes a void no time will fill up. If not the last, he was the *best* of the wits; and to myself his kindness and condescension were always extraordinary. I used to wonder at his not only sparing, but even sometimes being willing to seek me; and it is a sort of fond pleasure, that among the last books he read (forgive the vanity!) were my poor Musical Journals ("Music and Manners"), saying that he should like to know something about the matter.

Mitford, on her side, was not less interested in Chorley, as is shown by her frequent admiring and affectionate references to him in the first series of her published letters.* This series was the subject of an article from his pen in the 'Quarterly Review' (Jan. 1870); and one of his last literary labours was to edit a second series, with a brief memoir prefixed, which attests his feeling for the writer. Two or three personal touches therein are evidently drawn from reminiscences of his visits to Three Mile Cross: as, for example, the references made to her residence as an 'insufficient and meanly-furnished labourer's 'cottage,' the poverty of which was forced upon her by her father's extravagance, and only relieved by her 'one luxury—the tiny

---

* *Vide* vol. iii., *passim*, and especially p. 55. "My friend, Mr. Chorley, who is, I am very sorry to say, going away to-morrow, will be the bearer of my letter and of a few flowers; and if he have the good luck to be let in, as I hope he may, will tell you all about our doings. He is worthy of the pleasure of seeing you, not merely in right of admiration of your poems, but because he is one of the most perfectly right-minded and high-minded persons that I have ever known." (Letter to Miss Barrett, June, 1836.)

' flower-garden,' with its geraniums and ' the
' great bay-tree, beneath which so many distin-
' guished persons have congregated, to talk
' of matters far above and beyond the petty
' gossip of a country neighbourhood, or the
' private trials and sacrifices of their quiet
' hostess.'

Such letters from her as he has retained—
some of which might be worth adding to complete the collection of her published correspondence—evince alike her high appreciation
of Chorley's literary ability, and the reliance
she placed upon his judgment in matters of
every-day concern. Reserving illustrations of
the one for a later chapter, I may illustrate
the other by inserting a letter which she
wrote to him on the subject of a contemplated change of residence. It has no date,
but must belong to the year 1842, when his
hymn on the Prince of Wales' birth was
written :

" MY DEAR FRIEND,

" I thank you most earnestly for your great kindness. Be quite sure that I will do nothing unadvisedly. We shall meet, I trust, and then we will talk the matter over; at all events, nothing is decided; and until Midsummer, I shall not make up my mind any way. There is before a committee of the House of Commons a proposition for a railway from Reading to Basingstoke. Whatever line is taken, whether just in front of my cottage or close behind the garden, you know enough of the *locale* to conceive the destruction of all prettiness, for the embankment would be higher than this house. Then we should lose the coaches and post-carts, which, now that I have parted with my pony-chaise, are so necessary; and even if the railway were not to take place, the house and garden are too expensive. Under these considerations, what is there wonderful in my being tempted by a place so cheap and so very beautiful—where there is an excellent town, admirable libraries, French and English, and fair society; weather neither hot nor cold; dry winter walks (the dirt here has been frightful!) and a climate not more moist than that of the West of England? Very many of my friends have been there, and all speak of Jersey (for, on account of the excellence of the town, we should prefer that island to Guernsey)—all speak of Jersey as a very delightful residence, and, in point of vegetation, something unapproachable in this part of the world. Only think of an avenue of blue hydrangeas ten or twelve feet high, and large in proportion! I don't care so much for them; but think, where they so flourish, what may be expected from the fuschias, myrtles, camellias, and geraniums? Ah! you must come and see me there. I shall live a mile or two from St. Heliers, and you may be as retired there as in any part of Germany. You know that there is always a better chance of seeing you out of England than in. I have had for the last six weeks an abominable attack of rheumatism in the face, which will prevent my hearing Mr. Hullah's lecture to-morrow night at Reading—Mr. Risfield having had the goodness to offer me tickets. I regret this more as I should have liked to hear your beautiful hymn for the Prince of Wales. How very beautiful those verses are! What do you think of Mr. Horne's book—eh? How I do want a chat with you! When is the opera to come out? I see no newspapers, so know nothing on the subject.

" Heaven bless you, my dear friend,

" Ever faithfully yours,

" M. MITFORD."

To Miss Mitford's introduction he was indebted for some of the most valued of his literary acquaintances and personal friendships—notably those which he formed with John Kenyon, William Harness, the family of Charles Kemble, George Darley, Mr. Justice Talfourd, Mr. Browning, and, at a somewhat later period, with the illustrious poetess who became Mr. Browning's wife. Of Chorley's intimacies with Kenyon and Harness he has recorded little ; but he never mentions either without a tribute to the genuine kindliness of heart and refinement of mind which he prized in both. For the brilliant sisters, Mrs. Butler and Mrs. Sartoris, his admiration was only exceeded by his regard. With the former he frequently corresponded, and has preserved several of her letters ; but the privacy of such communications must be observed in this as in all cases where his correspondents are living, and have not sanctioned their publication. The names of George Darley, and Mr. Justice Talfourd have already been coupled together by Chorley in a passage of reminiscence, as connected with an untoward incident early in his literary career. Had he continued the narrative, he would, doubtless, have referred to the friendly relations that subsequently existed between himself and both. From Darley—to whose remarkable attainments in the contrasted spheres of poetry, criticism, and mathematics the world has yet, perhaps, hardly done justice — he has preserved two letters, both characteristic of the writer, and testifying to his appreciation of a kindred spirit in his correspondent. They are undated, but belong to the period between 1836 and 1846:

" 27, Upper Eaton Street,
" 16th August.

" MY DEAR SIR,

" Forgive me when I confess that, most ignorantly and unjustly thinking you altogether devoted to the popular literature of the day, and that little sympathy could, therefore, exist between us, I have let pass opportunities for cultivating your acquaintance. Miss Mitford, by her letter, has shown me how far I was mistaken. My error will be excused, I have no doubt, as freely as it is acknowledged. Yours can be no common mind, to be in such amity with hers. I regret my inability to give you any better proof of my conversion than the accompanying little pamphlet of a poem,* printed for friends; but the same en-

---

* Entitled " Nepenthe."

couraging spirit tells me it will not be un-
acceptable. Some friends have complained,
naturally enough, that an incomplete poem
is rather unintelligible. I have, therefore, written explanatory headings; and
may here add what is the general object
or mythos of the poem : viz., to show the
folly of discontent with the natural tone
of human life. Canto I. attempts to paint
the ill-effects of over-joy; Canto II., those
of excessive melancholy. Part of the latter
object remains to be worked out in Canto III.,
which would likewise show — if I could
ever find confidence, and health, and leisure to finish it—that contentment with the
mingled cup of humanity is the true 'Nepenthe.' I would call, or ask you to call, but
that conversation with me is a painful effort,
and to others painful and profitless. I am an
involuntary misanthrope, by reason of an impediment which renders society and me bur-
thensome to each other. My works, whatever be their merit, are the better part of
me—the only one I can at all commend to

your notice.   I alone have to regret my state of interdiction.

" Yours, my dear Sir,
" With respect and the best impressions towards you,
" GEORGE DARLEY."

" Thursday.

" MY DEAR CHORLEY,

" All my best thanks for your kind and careful remarks, which shall have my deepest consideration.   They are the only ones I have ever yet obtained which enable me to turn my mind upon itself.   Would they had come before I was dead in hope, energy, and ambition!   If the 'Lämmergeyer' now ten years old, be ever published, it will owe to you much of any success it may obtain, though I have not the slightest belief it will ever take even a 'very *low* place among our select romantic poems.'   You are perfectly right about 'Alboin.'   The simple truth is, it was written as a mock-heroic tragedy, called 'The Revisal,' by an imaginary mad dramatist, with a running prose critique by a manager, in which all your opinions of it were given. I, however, thought this plan foolish, and put one act into its present form, merely as an experiment, because it seemed to contain some few good lines. Whenever you please to put me in the chair, I promise to be as sincere as you, though not so judicious. Being such near neighbours, I think we should try the extent of each other's hospitality. Mine goes as far as a breakfast of tea and coffee, two eggs (or an equivalent broil), and buttered rolls *ad libitum.* Will you come Saturday, and at what hour? Or shall I put *your* ' barbarian virtue ' to the test, as you are upon the *first floor?*

" Ever yours obliged,

" GEORGE DARLEY.

" Had you rather have an *evening rout?*"

Of the author of " Ion " Chorley seems to have known less than of the critic, for whose severity on it he was so unreasonably held responsible. The misunderstanding, however, between himself and Talfourd on that score was soon rectified; and to prevent any recurrence of it, on the next occasion that a volume by so sensitive an author received unfavourable review from the 'Athenæum,' Chorley, as may be inferred from the following letter, took the pains to send him a previous disavowal. The absence of a date renders it impossible to identify the volume referred to.

"Court of C. P.
"Saturday evening.

"My dear Sir,

"I read your note last night with great regret; not for the anticipated article in the 'Athenæum,' but for the pain you have suffered entirely without other cause than your own sensibility and kindness. I assure you that I should have perfectly understood the true state of the case in reference to yourself, on a glance at the review; for it has happened to me, when writing dramatic criticisms for the 'New Monthly,' not merely to see my friends attacked by the editor, but to have my own article of eulogy altered into censure. I have just skimmed over the article this morning, and while I am ready to admit a great deal of it to be very just, I am surprised at a tone of personality, which I am afraid must have been excited by some offence I have unconsciously given to the writer. I have, however, so great an excess of praise to be grateful for in other quarters, that I should be inexcusable if I murmured at a censure which I may feel in some respects unjust. If disengaged, will you look in upon us on Sunday (to-morrow) evening, in Russell Square? You will find Miss Mitford and Mr. Kenyon, and one or two others, who, like myself, only wish to know you better.

"Ever faithfully yours,

"T. N. TALFOURD."

For Mr. Browning Chorley entertained the highest possible admiration, and their intimacy was for many years on a most cordial footing. In subsequent chapters I shall more than once have occasion to illustrate this, in connection with Chorley's literary labours, by extracts from two or three characteristic letters addressed to him by Mr. Browning, which I have been kindly permitted to print.

Another illustrious friendship which Chorley formed during these years was with the late George Grote. How they first became acquainted does not appear, but his name occurs in Chorley's journal as early as 1839, and the terms upon which they stood with each other a year or two later were evidently very intimate. Of this eminent man he has left the following notice, which worthily attests the value which he set upon their intercourse :

' The Historian of Greece, one of the few
' serious English men of letters who has made
' his mark all the world over, within the past
' half century, was for many years indulgently
' kind to me. A more noble-hearted and ac-
' complished gentleman than he who has
' departed full of years, and rich in honours, I
' have never seen. When the word " gentle-
' " man " is used, it is with express reference
' to that courtesy and consideration of manner,
' which appears to me dying out of the world.

' Four men that I have known, the late Duc
' de Grâmont, the Duke of· Ossuna, the late
' Duke of Beaufort, and Mr. Grote, in their
' high breeding and deference to women, in
' their instinctive avoidance of any topic or
' expression which could possibly give pain,
' recur to me as unparagoned. But the three
' men first named had little beyond their
' manner by way of charming or influencing
' society.* Mr. Grote, as a man holding those
' most advanced ideas which were at war with
' every aristocratic tradition and institution, a
' man with vigorous purposes, and ample and
' various stores of thought, might well have
' been allowed to dispense with form, and
' smoothness, and ceremony. But he showed

* ' Yet the Spanish grandee could at once evade and
' rebuke a piece of noble English impertinence. Rumour had
' exaggerated the extent of the Duke's fortune and posses-
' sions; but they were notoriously very large—for Spain. I
' heard an Earl, whose name should have been a warrant for
' good taste and good breeding, ask him point blank, " What
' " was the amount of his income?"—there being, if I remem-
' ber rightly, a wager at Crockford's to be settled by the
' answer. "My lord," said the Duke, with the most imper-
' turbable politeness, "I do not know your English money." '

' how these could be combined with the most
' utter sincerity. If, at times, he was elaborate
' in conversation, with little humour of expres-
' sion, though not without a sense of it in
' others, he was never overweening. He
' stands in a place of his own, among all
' the superior men to whom I have ever
' looked up.

   ' He was a sceptic, as regards matters of
' religious faith, to the very core. But he was
' keenly alive to the truth, that to force
' extreme opinions, not called for, on those
' having other convictions, is an abuse of
' freedom of thought and of speech which
' no large-minded man will permit himself.
' There was neither craft nor cowardice in this
' reticence. Had fortune, or wordly position,
' or life, depended on his falsifying his
' opinions, he is the last man I have ever
' known who would have done so. His
' uncompromising constancy to his peculiar
' opinions cost him all influence and support
' in Parliament, and was the cause of his early
' retirement from political life and action.

' With all his vast stores of knowledge, and
' his habits of universal reading, were com-
' bined a taste for Art, and a certain amount
' of practical accomplishment not common
' among scholars so profound and so ripe. He
' was a lover rather than a judge of pictures;
' he was an intelligent opera-goer, and had
' made some proficiency in learning to play on
' the violoncello. But in everything he under-
' took, whether it was of grave importance
' or of slighter pastime, his modesty was as
' remarkable as his earnestness and his cour-
' tesy. The completeness of the scholar and
' the gentleman strikes me more forcibly on
' retrospect than it did at the time when I was
' frequently in his society. It is fit that he
' should lie among the high-minded and let-
' tered men who have made England great
' among the nations. But even were there no
' stone in the Abbey to hand his merits down
' for scholars and politicians to come to imitate,
' I am satisfied that his reputation will only
' brighten and deepen as years pass on, and
' new men take up the studies in which his

' honourable life was spent; and the result
' of which has already a wide and lasting
' place in the world of letters.'

The only other names that can be added to
the list of Chorley's literary intimacies of this
period, are those of William and Mary Howitt.
They were friends of his family, and his acquaintance with them, which had preceded
his arrival in London, always partook rather
of a domestic than of a personal character.
Observing the rule already prescribed in
cases where the living are subjects of reference, I shall only say that he was in occasional correspondence with Mrs. Howitt on
topics of common interest, and at various
times her guest for several days together.

The friendships comprised in this *aurea
catena* were for the most part formed and
maintained concurrently. They, doubtless,
varied considerably in degree, but none of
them equalled in intensity the bond which
had united him to Mr. Benson Rathbone,
nor weakened the force of the domestic associations with which that early friendship

was incorporated. Although necessarily debarred from much intercourse with his family at Liverpool,* Chorley's affection for them was undiminished. They habitually corresponded, and such intervals of leisure as he could afford were spent in their circle. Now and then he seems to have complained

---

* In this connection I must not omit to notice his indebtedness to the wife of Mr. Dilke for the motherly interest 'she took in him from the time of his engagement on the 'Athenæum,' the many acts of thoughtful kindness by which the sense of exile that might have oppressed him in the first years of his London life was effectually dissipated. That Chorley was not unmindful of her consideration is shown by several of his letters that have been preserved, and of which the following is a pleasant sample :—

"DEAR MRS. DILKE,

"You are to fancy yourself a day younger, or the almanac wrong, that I may have the pleasure of begging your acceptance of a little birthday token to wish you as much happiness as you give—and especially to remind you that I am now in that article ten years in your debt. I must always remain so, I fear, for an amount of cheerful and unwearied kindness which has thrown the charm of home over my London life. But pray, sometimes, when you put on the little trinket, remember that the obligation is gratefully and affectionately owned, though it cannot be repaid, by

"Your faithful and obliged,

"HENRY F. CHORLEY.

"Feb. 2, 1844."

of the imperfect sympathy with his interests which was displayed by some of its members, principally his brother John, who afterwards came to know him better; but with one of them at least, his sister, he was in uninterrupted accord, and there is often a suffusion of chivalric tenderness in the phrases he employs in connection with her name. Two deaths that occurred in these years left a void in his own home, and that of another family only less dear to him. In October, 1838, he was summoned to the death-bed of his uncle, Dr. Rutter, whom he revered as a second father; and Mrs. Rathbone, who occupied an almost maternal place in his affection, died in the following May. By the death of the former his mother was left in affluent circumstances, and he became entitled to a legacy of 1400*l.*—an addition to his slender means as timely as it was grateful.

Among the remarkable persons moving in London society at the time when he entered it, and whom he met and observed frequently without ever knowing intimately, was

the poet and banker, Rogers. Of him Chorley
has left a sketch, which, though necessarily
slight and superficial, contains some characteristic traits.

‘ I used to meet Rogers frequently at the
‘ Grotes’, at the Kembles’, at the Procters’;
‘ and at the first house in very small parties,
‘ where I had an opportunity of hearing and
‘ seeing him closely. Few old men have ever
‘ shown a more mortifying behaviour to a
‘ young one than Mr. Rogers, from the first to
‘ the last, displayed towards me. There was
‘ no doubting the dislike which he had con-
‘ ceived for me, and which he took every
‘ possible pains to make me feel. I do not
‘ recollect ever to have intruded myself on his
‘ notice, ever to have interrupted him in narra-
‘ tion (an offence which he could not endure).
‘ In the society where I met him I never
‘ talked, for it was a delight to listen to
‘ Sydney Smith, and to Charles Austin, and
‘ to Mr. and Mrs. Grote. Perhaps Rogers
‘ thought my dress coxcombical, or my manner
‘ affected, (an accusation under which I have

' lain all my life). Perhaps he did not forgive
' me for living as house-mate with a person
' for whom he openly professed antipathy.
' Whatever the cause might be, he did his
' best to make me feel small and uncomfort-
' able; and it was often done by repeating
' the same discouragement. The scene would
' be a dinner of eight; at which he would say,
' loud enough to be heard, " Who is that
' " young man with red hair ?" (meaning me).
' The answer would be, " Mr. Chorley," *et*
' *cetera, et cetera.* " Never heard of him
' " before," was the rejoinder: after which
' Rogers would turn to his dinner, like one
' who, having disposed of a nuisance, might
' unfold his napkin, and eat his soup in peace.

' It has been fortunate for me all my life
' that unprovoked rudeness of this sort has
' never had any power over me, has never
' added to a physical nervousness, of itself
' sufficiently disqualifying, nor to a shyness,
' which I don't think has included moral
' cowardice. Those to whom I have attached
' myself, and those in whom I have believed,

‘ have been able to give me any amount of
‘ pain. I have been hag-ridden all my life by
‘ an over-sensitiveness with respect to *friends*,
‘ and have suffered from my own jealous and
‘ exacting nature, from too much yearning for
‘ entire confidence and complete regard. But
‘ slights from acquaintances I have never
‘ heeded, more than I should heed a random
‘ call at my heels in the street. And thus the
‘ deliberate and avowed antipathy of Mr.
‘ Roger (never provoked by want of respect
‘ on my part) served only to amuse me, as a
‘ trait of character, and did not prevent my
‘ profiting, as well as I could, by all that was
‘ more genial in his nature and manners. It
‘ still seems to me a doubtful matter which of
‘ the two attributes was reality, which affecta-
‘ tion ; the elegance and sympathy and deli-
‘ cacy he could throw into his intercourse
‘ with those whom he protected, or the acer-
‘ bity, often displayed and directed without
‘ any conceivable reason, with which he pur-
‘ sued unaffected persons, or denounced every-
‘ thing in literature and art which did not

' suit him. His admiration, in some points
' showing a marvellous foresight, in others,
' hung so curiously far behind his time, as to
' puzzle all those who are apt to dream that
' liberality should exclude prejudice. As a
' young man collecting pictures, he showed
' an excellent courage in leaving all the beaten
' tracks of connoisseurship, to select, and enjoy,
' and recognise that which he felt to be good.
' He was one of the first in England who
' recognised ancient Italian painting, as
' having a beauty and an expression totally
' distinct from archæological value; not re-
' pelled by technical mistakes or audacities,
' provided the work was sincere. But as an
' old poet, who was ever so inhuman and
' perverse in sitting in judgment on the works
' of young poets as Rogers? I have heard
' him absolutely venomous and violent (as
' much as so low-voiced a man could be) in
' dissection, or in wholesale abuse, of the
' verses of Tennyson, Browning, Milnes; and
' end his task of " perverse industry," (as
' Moore has somewhere happily designated

' such exhibitions) with such a sigh of satis-
' faction as might befit one to whom the
' extermination of vermin is not a profession,
' but a pleasure.

' In music, too, he was no less exclusive,
' no less vicious in reproof, but far more
' ignorant. How one, who had been hearing
' music for so many years, and who would
' never keep away from any place where it
' was going on, 'could have made so little
' progress in taste and knowledge as Rogers,
' used to excite my wonderment. Scott, it is
' said, used to profess that he was totally
' devoid of musical sense, save such as enabled
' him to bear the burden to Mrs. Lockhart's
' ballads, or to sing after supper (as Moore
' has told) over the quaigh of whisky. But
' I cannot but imagine that Rogers, with all
' his profession, was as meagrely gifted by
' nature as Scott had been, and that his
' culture had merely been applied to the fos-
' tering of those old associative prejudices
' which, however precious as pleasures of
' memory, have nothing to do with the good

' or ill of music. The name of Beethoven
' used to make him singularly active and
' acrid in epithet: instrumental music, of any
' kind, was " *those fiddlers;*" though he would
' lavish gracious compliments on a Kemble,
' an Arkwright, or a Grisi, or any woman
' who sung, no matter what, small matter
' how, she sung. It was on the debateable
' land of music that I used to meet Mr. Rogers
' the most frequently, since he came to many
' houses which I frequented, ostensibly to hear
' and to enjoy music; and, sometimes, for the
' sake of getting a name or a fact, would even
' lay by his antipathy and ignorance of me,
' and ask, "*What was going on?*" or, "*where-*
' *abouts we were?*" I remember one night in
' particular, his religiously sitting through a
' fine performance of Beethoven's Mass in C,
' and pertinaciously appealing to me, from
' movement to movement, "*Now, is that good?*
' *—because I don't know!*" "*Now, do you*
' *really understand that?*"

' The temptation to retort was strong:
' " What need to sit ?"—till one recollected

‘ the different world into which he had been
‘ born, the different atmosphere as regards
‘ Art, which he had breathed ; and admitted
‘ that the good of his willingness to listen
‘ ought to outweigh the bad of his arrogance
‘ in knocking down all that he could not
‘ understand.

‘ And very great and very bitter was that
‘ arrogance. One night Mrs. Sartoris had
‘ been singing a canzonet by Signor ——,
‘ who had accompanied her. When it was
‘ done, Rogers made the labour of crossing
‘ the room and going up to the pianoforte ;
‘ “ What was that you have been singing ?”
‘ said he, in his low, clear voice. “ A song
‘ “ of Signor ——,” was the answer ; “ give
‘ “ me leave to introduce him to you.” “ I
‘ “ thought it was that man’s !” was the
‘ gracious reply ; “ *there’s no tune in it.*”

‘ I have always considered myself the person
‘ to whom Rogers made his most gratuitously
‘ ill-natured speech, as under. It was at the
‘ *Antient Concerts*, on a night when the room
‘ was crowded, owing to a royal visit, and

' when every seat was occupied. Mine was
' at the end of a bench, by the side of the
' Dowager Lady Essex (Miss Stephens that
' had been). She was one of Rogers' prime
' favourites; even though she is in private as
' in public one of those gracious and gentle
' women against whom no exception can be
' taken. He loved to sit next her, and pay
' her those elegant and courteous compliments,
' the art of paying which is lost. When I
' saw the old gentleman creeping down the
' side avenue betwixt the benches, at a loss
' for a seat, I said, *"Now I shall give up my*
' *" place to Mr. Rogers; good-night."* While I
' was stooping for my hat, " Come," said she,
' in her cordial way, " come, Mr. Rogers, here
' is a seat for you by me." " Thank you,"
' said the civil old gentleman, fixing his dead
' eyes on me, as I was doing my best to get
' out of the way; " thank you; *but I don't*
' *like your company."*
  ' I may tell a companion story which I
' heard from the younger Westmacott the
' sculptor, who was rather a favourite with

‘ Rogers than otherwise. Westmacott had
‘ finished a bust, I believe, of Lord John
‘ Russell, and, being anxious that Lord John’s
‘ friends should pronounce on the likeness,
‘ invited Mr. Rogers to his *studio* with that
‘ express view. The poet, I suppose, came on
‘ a bad day, for round and round the room he
‘ walked, and through and through the laby-
‘ rinth of marbles, slowly and ponderingly,
‘ passing the bust in a marked manner. At
‘ last he paused, paused before one of those
‘ *hunches* of marble which have only begun to
‘ assume human semblance, by the drill holes
‘ and compass marks with which the sculptor’s
‘ men prepare the block for the sculptor’s own
‘ chisel. Here he stopped and pointed with
‘ his finger, “ *I think,*” said he, “ *that’s the best*
‘ “ *likeness here.*”

‘ Though I have done my best to produce
‘ a true picture of the humours of the Rogers
‘ I saw and met often, let me no less earnestly
‘ state my belief that the crookedness and the
‘ incivility of these had nothing to do with his
‘ heart and his hand, when the one told the

‘ other to give. Rogers’ hospitality to poets
‘ might be pleasant to himself, and no less so
‘ his handsome reception of every handsome
‘ woman, but for the poor, struggling, suffer-
‘ ing man of genius, and to the garret with
‘ its dirt and cold, without any charm, or
‘ warmth, or Southern picturesque, he was,
‘ I believe, a delicate almoner, a liberal dis-
‘ tributor, and a frequent visitor. Bilious,
‘ vicious, *cruel* as he was with his tongue,
‘ Rogers was, I know, a kindly and inde-
‘ fatigable friend to many humble men, and
‘ to a few less humble ones; and at no period
‘ of his life, when his antipathy to me was the
‘ most rancorously expressed, should I have
‘ feared presenting to him the case of poor
‘ painter, poor poet, poor musician, or poor
‘ governess. Though I never *did* apply to
‘ Rogers for aid to others, I am personally
‘ cognizant of too many acts of munificence
‘ quietly done by him, and of which no trum-
‘ peting was or *is* possible, not to dwell on
‘ the good as warmly as I talk about the
‘ mischief unreservedly.’

Of another celebrity of the same period, the late Lady Morgan, Chorley knew somewhat more than of Rogers. They used occasionally to correspond, and one of her letters to him is subjoined to the following estimate which he has left of her character.

'One of the most peculiar and original ' literary characters whom I have ever known, ' was Sydney Lady Morgan, a composition of ' natural genius, acquired accomplishments, ' audacity that flew at the highest game, ' shrewd thought, and research at once intelli- ' gent and superficial ; personal coquetries and ' affectations, balanced by sincere and strenu- ' ous family affections; extreme liberality of ' opinions, religious and political; extremely ' narrow literary sympathies, united with a ' delight in all the most tinsel pleasures and ' indulgences of the most inane aristocratic ' society ; a genial love for Art, limited by ' the most inconceivable prejudices of ignor- ' ance ; in brief, a compound of the most ' startling contradictions, impossible to be ' overlooked or forgotten, though possible to

' be described in two ways—both true, yet the
' one diametrically opposite to the other.
' Those whom she exasperated by her scep-
' ticism and her fearlessness of speech and
' action, could only dwell upon her frivolity
' and vanity, which were patent enough;
' those whose tempers were not heated by
' rivalry or antagonism could discern beneath
' all these fopperies a solidity of conviction,
' a sincerity of purpose, and a constancy of re-
' gard which could not fail to win apprecia-
' tion of, though they could not always ensure
' respect for their owner. Her life, were it
' thoroughly and truly told, would be one of
' the most singular contributions to the history
' of gifted woman that the world has ever
' seen. She tried to tell it herself, in a frag-
' mentary fashion, from time to time; but the
' chapters of a strange story, however amus-
' ing, were like their writer, so made up and
' rouged for effect as not to have taken a
' permanent place in the library of Female
' Biographies. It may be doubted whether
' such a woman will be ever seen again, since

' many of her peculiarities were clearly ascrib-
' able to circumstances of birth and education,
' which, in our days of rapid intercourse and
' diffused instruction, can hardly be repro-
' duced.   The efforts of the young to acquire
' distinction must henceforth take other milder
' forms than they formerly wore, must be more
' speculative, less practical : on the other hand,
' perhaps, the distinction when gained will
' never be so original and direct in its mani-
' festation, nor so racy in its expression, in
' any generation to come.

  ' Lady Morgan, when touched too closely
' on the subject of her birth, was used to say,
' that she was born on the sea, betwixt Ire-
' land and England.   I have heard her declare
' in one breath that she had created the
' national Irish novel, while in another, with
' sublime inconsistency, she would assert that
' Miss Edgeworth was a grown woman when
' she was yet a child.   Her father, Mr. Mac-
' owen (the name for gentility's sake legiti-
' mately transformed into Owenson) was a
' comic actor of some repute in Ireland, some

‘ eighty or a hundred years ago. I have
‘ always believed that Sydney, his daughter,
‘ was destined for public exhibition, as she
‘ was taught to sing, to dance, to recite, and
‘ to play on the harp. But in none of these
‘ accomplishments was she sufficiently tutored
‘ to make limited natural gifts and per-
‘ sonal attractions presentable to that hard
‘ taskmaster, the Public, with any chance of
‘ great favour. And the girl early discovered
‘ that she had within herself better chances
‘ of asserting her individuality; a shrewd ob-
‘ servation of character, a keen wit, a fearless
‘ tongue, a resolute desire and curiosity for
‘ instruction in the ways of the world. Any-
‘ thing but regularly pretty, she must at one
‘ time have been odd and piquant looking; in
‘ this more attractive than many a dull com-
‘ pound of lilies and roses.

‘ The resolution to get on rarely fails to be
‘ its own fulfilment. From the moment when
‘ she was received into the Marquis of Aber-
‘ corn’s family, partly as a governess, partly
‘ as a household musician, her success in the

' life she coveted and was fittest for, became
' only a matter of time. She danced, she
' played on the harp ; by her mother-wit she
' amused the inane persons of quality whom,
' in later years, she delighted so mercilessly
' to satirise in her novels. But all this time
' she was reading eagerly in a desultory
' fashion ; getting some superficial knowledge
' of French and Italian ; if without any very
' steady purpose, with that instinct of future
' success which contains the fulfilment of its
' own prophecy.

' There is no need to dwell on Lady Mor-
' gan's first attempts at fiction ; " Ida of
' " Athens," " The Novice of St. Dominick,"
' " The Wild Irish Girl," the last probably
' the least imitative, the one which gave to
' its writer her own pet name of Glorvina,
' after its heroine. All are as much for-
' gotten as the tale " St. Irvyne," by which
' Shelley began his literary career. A
' collection of Irish Melodies, long preced-
' ing those of Bunting and Moore, was of
' better promise. One of these, " Kate

' Kearney," still lives in cheap editions of
' popular songs.

   ' It is as little my business to offer any
' judgment here on Lady Morgan's National
' Tales; neither on her travels in France and
' Italy, her " Life of Salvator Rosa," and the
' most serious and best of her works, " Woman
' " and her Master." Whatever be their real
' merit, it is past doubt that they established
' for her a brilliant reputation in France and
' Italy, and this expressed in forms which
' were not calculated to give ballast to one of
' the most feather-brained, restless creatures
' who ever glittered in the world of female
' authorship. After her first book on " France "
' was published she became the *rage* in Paris;
' and I have been told, on good authority, that
' on one occasion, at some grand reception, she
' had a raised seat on the *dais*, only a little
' lower than that provided for the Duchesse de
' Berri. It is true that she had at her side a
' staid, shrewd, cynical, sceptical companion
' in Sir Charles Morgan, who was weary of
' bearing a part in perpetual glitter, his mind

' being bent on graver pursuits and specula-
' tions than hers. A strangely assorted pair
. ' they seemed to be, on a first glance; but the
' one suited the other admirably. He did
' something towards reducing the exuberances
' of her vanity, and directing her attention to
' courses of research. That he helped to write
' her books, as has been asserted, I do not
' believe. Her fame, for it amounted to fame,
' gave him access to circles of society which
' possibly he might never otherwise have
' entered. Both agreed in the expression of
' the most fearless scepticism (sometimes most
' painfully and needlessly expressed); both,
' like all the sceptics I have ever approached,
' were absurdly prejudiced and proof against
' new impressions. Neither of them, though
' both were literary and musical, could endure
' German literature or music, had got beyond
' the stale sarcasms of the " Anti-Jacobin," or
' could admit that there is a glory for such
' men as Weber, Beethoven, Mendelssohn, as
' well as for Cimarosa, Paiesiello, and Rossini.
'. Prejudice such as theirs, professing liberal-

' ism, is a " sure card " to play. Party ani-
' mosity is far more amusing than justice, the
' latter being apt to bear the bad name of
' phlegmatic indifference. He, however anti-
' pathetic his views might be to many persons,
' was, I have no doubt, thoroughly sincere in
' them; she was as much so as a spoilt woman
' of genius, who delighted in being thought
' a woman of fashion, could be.

  ' Her familiar conversation was a series of
' brilliant, egotistic, shrewd, genial sallies.
' She could be caressing or impudent, as
' suited the moment, the purpose in hand, or
' the person she was addressing. At times
' the generous, hearty nature of the Irish-
' woman broke out, strangely alternating with
' her love of show and finery, and the bitter
' cynicism she showered on all practices and
' opinions which rebuked her own. I recol-
' lect her telling how, when she had been
' detained at some road-side country inn by
' an illness of her husband's, she sat on the
' bench beside the door, and treated a party
' of weary country labourers, who were there

' resting, to bread, cheese, and beer, having
' obviously taken a rich and real enjoyment
' in their homely talk.   And the next mo-
' ment she would fly off to some nonsense
' about dukes and duchesses, royal celebrities,
' at home and abroad, who had complimented
' her books, her conversation, or her toilette;
' for of her toilette, which was largely, during
' her life, made by her own hands, she was
' comically vain without concealment. I re-
' member to have heard her describe a party
' at a *Mrs. Leo Hunter's*, (who received all
' manner of celebrities at what she called " her
' " morning *soirées*," without the slightest
' power of appreciating anything but the
' celebrity)—" There," said she, " was Miss
' " Jane Porter, looking like a shabby canon-
' " ess; there was Mrs. Somerville, in an
' " astronomical cap. *I* dashed in, in my blue
' " satin and point-lace, and showed them how
' " an authoress should dress."

' I remember her, at another of those won-
' drous gatherings, where the crowd was
' great, and the drawing-room was crammed,

' breaking through a company of men, who
' had perched on an upper staircase, sitting
' down, and crying out aloud, " Here I am in
' " the midst of my seraglio!"   In freedom of
' speech she proved herself the countrywoman
' of those renowned wits, Lady Norbury and
' Lady Aldborough ; but, however free, she
' never shocked decorum, as they rather re-
' joiced in doing, to have their tales of *double*
' *entendre* carted over the town by diners
' out, who found the second-hand indecency
' answer, as creating " a sensation."

' What a blessing is self-approbation !   In
' Lady Morgan's case I am satisfied it was
' sincere.   She had no Statute of Limitations,
' and absolutely professed to have taught
' Taglioni to dance an Irish jig !   How far
' Taglioni profited by the lesson is a secret.

' Sometimes " her spirit and vivacity " (as
' the inimitable Lady Strange expressed it)
' carried Lady Morgan into strange lengths
' of freedom.   I once met her in a literary
' *ménagerie*, where, among other guests, figured
' a large lady, but a small authoress, Mrs.

' Cornwell Baron Wilson. She displayed
' rather protuberantly, below the waist of
' her black dress, a tawdry medal, half the
' size of a saucer, which had been awarded
' her for some prize poems by some provincial
' Della Cruscan literary society, probably
' as tawdry and of as little worth as the
' rhymes it was given to reward. " My
' " ——!" said Lady Morgan, using an excla-
' mation more irreverent than the reverse,
' " only look at Grace Darling !" (the heroic
' daughter of the Northern Lighthouse-
' keeper). "Hush! hush!" said some one or
' other, "It is Mrs. Cornwell Baron Wilson."
' " Who ? Oh, Mrs. Barry Cornwall." I do
' not believe that she ever took the trouble to
' set her knowledge right regarding a lady
' living and moving in her own literary
' world. Yet who could be so sarcastic as
' herself on the mistakes of others ?

' I heard her ask, in all sincerity and
' simplicity, at a literary party, " Who was
' " Jeremy Taylor ?" on the occasion of some
' reference to that distinguished divine. She

' may have, and I think had, some notion of
' the Taylors of Ongar!   But more absurd
' still was her introduction to the stately,
' grave, and accomplished Mrs. Sarah Austin,
' on which occasion she complimented her
' sister authoress on having written " Pride
' " and Prejudice."

' Her resolution to assemble lions of all
' sorts and sexes was nothing short of daunt-
' less.   If a nobody happened to get into her
' circle, she made no scruple to pass him or her
' off as "; the Cleopatra pears " were passed off
' by my relative. I think, could it have helped
' one of her parties, she would have fitted up
' a " Grace Darling."   I know of one quiet and
' unobtrusive woman whom she had invited,
' and subsequently thought it necessary to
' ticket, who overheard how she was pointed
' out by the hostess " as a woman of extraordi-
' " nary genius, who had written— " Well,
' the rest did not come easily, and so Lady
' Morgan fluttered off elsewhere, having mys-
' teriously accounted for the presence of an
' anonymous guest.

' Among the guests whom she received in
' her latter years, when the death of Sir Charles
' Morgan left her at liberty to consult her
' humours without restraint, was the last person
' whom one could have expected to meet within
' precincts such as hers—Cardinal Wiseman.
' Not long before had she written her pamphlets
' on St. Peter's chair at Rome, aimed at the
' immaculate immutability of Papal succession;
' papers controversial, as strong, and caustic,
' and conclusive, as possibly were ever written
' by a woman, in which she took great delight,
' (for her avowed pleasure in her own works
' was wonderful). I believe *his* eminence and
' *her* eminence met on grounds of the most
' cordial good fellowship. Such an encounter
' tells well for the honest sense and real feel-
' ing of the conflicting parties. Such encoun-
' ters, I have often had reason to think, are
' nowhere so frequent as in England.

' She could be recklessly bitter in regard to
' other, especially other Irish, literary women.
' Her hatred to Lady Blessington had no
' bounds. In point and quality of authorship

' no sane person could for an instant think of
' comparing the two ; and the writer of " Flor-
' " ence Macarthy," and the " Life of Salvator
' " Rosa," might well have afforded to pass by
' the more colourless works of the lady of Gore
' House.   But there Gore House was ; and, in
' spite of the more austere and literary and
' political attractions of Holland House beyond
' it, Lady Blessington, by her grace, her sweet-
' ness, her admirable tact as the leader of
' society, and her no less admirable constancy,
' contrived, in spite of the most tremendous
' social disadvantages, to draw round her such
' a circle of men there, as I fancy will hardly
' be seen again.   Lady Holland hated her
' badly, but, I think, let her alone ; Lady
' Morgan could not let her alone. I have never
' heard venom, irony, and the implacable and
' caricatured statement of past mistakes heaped
' *Pelion-wise* on *Ossa*, even by woman on
' woman, so mercilessly, as by Lady Morgan
' in regard to Lady Blessington. And the
' former had the bad taste to assail the known
' friends of the latter with perpetual gibings

' and assaults. I have never been able (as
' other literary men can do) to partake of
' such miserable stories as these without a
' feeling of shame and discomfort; as un-
' able as, I hope, unwilling, to spoil society
' by wrangling, which must merge in honest
' animosity should unprovoked scandals be
circulated.

' As life passed on, these follies in some
' measure fell away from, or were tempered,
' in Lady Morgan. She accepted what was
' becoming to advanced years with a grace
' almost amounting to dignity, hardly to have
' been expected from one who had so long
' defied time, and who found herself almost
' alone in the world. She became quieter,
' more considerate, very attentive to younger
' people, and to rising talent. She had been
' spoiled by having had to work her way under
' difficult circumstances into a position which
' she improved into a success. She had been
' flattered, and was more accessible to flattery
' than ninety-nine out of a hundred women
' are. She had the consciousness of having

' conquered a place for herself and her family,
' which was bright, and, to some degree, solid,
' in the best society of England and the Con-
' tinent. Last and best of all, she had never
' to be appealed or apologised for, as a for-
' lorn woman of genius under difficulties. The
' pension which was granted to her in her latter
' days, and justly, as one who had done her best
' to see after the redress of Irish abuses, had
' not, I have reason to believe, been soli-
' cited.'

The following letter was evidently written in reply to one wherein Chorley had asked for materials to enable him to draw up the biographical sketch of Lady Morgan, which was to be included in his " Authors of England," referred to in a previous chapter.

"Kildare Street, March 21, 1837.

" DEAR MR. CHORLEY,

"I seize on a transient gleam of *eye-shine* to write you a few lines on a subject which Sir Charles (in his desire to keep *all literary purposes* and pursuits out of my way),

has only lately revealed to me, viz., that *my
'life'* is going to be written for the edifica-
tion of the public! Now, except by *divine
inspiration*, no one *could* write my life but
myself! and I have now neither light nor
ambition to do so. I have an enormous mass
of journals and correspondences by me, of
twenty-five years (from which, by-the-bye, I
extracted the 'Book of the Boudoir'); the
journals full of European events and anecdotes,
and many of the letters to and from most of
the European *notabilities* of the age, and in
three languages; but these all lie hermetically
sealed in a great coffer for the present: (what
would dear little Colburn give to peep in?)
They will contain *my life* and *times*—should
they ever be arranged, without adding a line.
Prince Puckler Muskau came into my *boudoir*
one day when I was looking over my journals,
and asked me the title of my MSS. I said,
'Ces sont des mémoires *par* moi-même, *pour*
moi-même,' and so he has announced them
in his book of errors! Now, my dear Mr.
Chorley, you are an honest as well as a clever

man; I take it, therefore, for granted you will see fair play, and keep clear of the thousand and one *liars or lies* which party spirit, literary envy, and Prince Calumny have published of me. I have some incidents and anecdotes in foreign and other journals which I will bring you, and that may be of use to you in your biographical sketch, and they are true and amusing, and I will answer any questions you put to me *honestly;* but I trust you will not publish anything till our arrival in London, which will be about the first week in, or perhaps, at furthest, the second, in April. On this subject I beg you will write to me *immediately.* I suppose you have heard that Mr. H. L. Bulwer has *jilted us* in the affair of the house. There *never was such* a disappointment, or such an *unbusiness*-like transaction. Do you know I think *you* might render us a *great service* by looking about in your own pretty neighbourhood for apartments for us, until we could look about us for ourselves. I should have no objection to old Bowden's Bird-cage for a time. I must release you from deciphering this scrawl, which I am writing *by guess,* and so good day.

" SYDNEY MORGAN."

"We are still very uneasy about dear Mr. Dilke: pray let us know your own *private* opinion. Pray write as soon as possible. I am not allowed to *read* or *write* a line; this horror is perpetrated by stealth. The moment I use my eyes the pain and weakness return. Colburn is impatient for my work ("Woman and her Master "), but alas !——

"Will you have the kindness to send the note to Mr. Dilke, and to put Mrs. Webster's in the *petite poste ?*"

The service requested of him was duly rendered by Chorley, and for awhile he and the Morgans were next-door neighbours in Stafford Row. Their intercourse cooled in later years, as his sketch intimates, but without involving any actual estrangement; and with one of Lady Morgan's nieces—Mrs. Inwood Jones—he remained to the last on the most cordial terms.

Another celebrity of this period with whom Chorley came in contact, was the ill-starred Miss Landon (L. E. L.). Of her original hostility to him, as a writer in the journal most successful as a rival to that of which she was the chief ornament, mention has already been made. A notice which he has left of his subsequent relations with her, will attest the generosity of his disposition, and furnish an example, only too rare, of the " amenities " of literary intercourse :—

' In spite of the miserably low standard of
' her literary morality, Miss Landon (for awhile
' put forward as Mrs. Hemans's rival) was meant
' for better things. She was incomplete, but
' she was worthy of being completed ; she was
' ignorant, but she was quick, and capable of
' receiving culture, had she been allowed a
' chance. If she was unrefined, it was because
' she had fallen into the hands of a coarse set
' of men—the Tories of a provincial capital—
' such as then made a noise and a flare in the
' " Noctes Ambrosianæ " of " Blackwood's Ma-
' gazine," second-hand followers of Lockhart

' and Professor Wilson, and Theodore Hook;
' the most noisy and most reprehensible of
' whom—and yet one of the cleverest—was
' Dr. Maginn. Not merely did they, at a very
' early period of the girl's career, succeed in
' bringing her name into a coarse repute, from
' which it never wholly extricated itself, but,
' by the ridiculous exaggeration of such natural
' gifts as she possessed, (no doubt accompanied
' by immediate gain), flattered her into the
' idea that small further cultivation was re-
' quired by one who could rank with a Baillie,
' a Tighe, a Hemans—if not their superior,
' at least their equal. Further, she was not
' fortunate in her home position, called on to
' labour incessantly for the support of those
' around her. All this resulted in what may
' be called a *bravado* in her intercourse with
' the public, which excited immense distaste
' among those who were not of the coterie to
' which she belonged.

' As years went on, the ephemeral success
' of Miss Landon's verses subsided: and, in-
' deed, she had rendered herself next to inca-

' pable of anything like a sustained effort,
' though some of her smaller lyrics were more
' earnest and more real in their sentiment and
' sweetness than her earlier love-tales and
' ditties had been. There was amendment,
' too, in her versification. She attempted
' drama, in the tragedy, I think, of " Castruc-
' " cio Castrucani," but without the smallest
' success. She wrote a volume of sacred verse,
' which was sentimental rather than serious.
' She took Annuals in hand, but the result
' was the same, and it must have been felt so
' by herself. At last she began to write imagi-
' native prose; and the coterie who supported
' her blew the trumpet before her first novel;
' " Romance and Reality," as no one would
' do now-a-days were a new Dickens, or a new
' Bulwer, on the threshold. But she held out
' bravely; wearing out life, and health, and
' hope, as all who work on ground which is
' not solid *must* do; bravely holding up those
' who looked to her for position and subsistence
' in life, and keeping up before such of the
' friends she retained, and such of the society

' as she mixed in sparingly, those hectic, hys-
' terical high-spirits, which are even more
' depressing to meet than any melancholy.
' There was a certain audacious brightness in
' her talk; but it was only false glitter, not
' real brilliancy; it was smart, not sound.

' The truth of Miss Landon's story and her
' situation had for some time oozed out; it was
' felt that her literary reputation had been
' exaggerated; that her social position was, so
' to say, not the pleasantest in the world. Those
' who had, in some measure, compromised her,
' were in no case to assist her; those who had
' stood aside, had become aware of the deep and
' real struggle and sorrow which had darkened
' her whole life, from its youth upwards, and
' the many, many pleas for forbearance implied
' in such knowledge.

' There came a time for the recognition of
' these. A relative of hers was proposed to
' fill an office, in the giving away of which
' literary men had some words to say. And he
' was unimpeachably eligible. He had rested
' on her support. It was right that her devo-

' tion to her own family should not be allowed
' to drag her down; that her literary industry
' should be recognised—especially now, when it
' was failing of its reward. It was felt among
' some of us, that, in this matter, there was a
' claim to be upheld. I had to see her on the
' subject. It was, for both of us, an awkward
' visit. She received me with an air of astonish-
' ment and bravado, talking with a rapid and
' unrefined frivolity, the tone and taste of which
' were most distasteful, and the flow difficult to
' interrupt. When, at last, I was allowed to
' explain my errand, the change was instant
' and painful. She burst into a flood of hys-
' terical tears. 'Oh!" she cried, " you don't
' know the ill-natured things I have written
' about you!" From that time I saw her occa-
' sionally, and am satisfied of the sincerity of
' her feelings. Then, I came to perceive how
' much of what was good and real in her
' nature had been strangled and poisoned by
' the self-interested thoughtlessness of those
' who should have shielded her. Some grow-
' ing conviction of this it was, I have always

' thought, which drove her into a desire for
' escape, and this into her marriage.   It seemed
' next to impossible that the husband she chose
' could have anything in common with her.
' Her melancholy death (curiously foresha-
' dowed in her " Ethel Churchill "), painfully
' sudden as it was, may have delivered her
' from heart-ache and weariness to come. But
' her ill-fortune pursued her after the catas-
' trophe at Cape Coast Castle, caused by her
' mistake of one medicine for another.   It
' would be worse than fruitless to rake up the
' scandals to which this gave rise, and which
' had their usual complement of malicious
' listeners. " Very sorrowful," says the author,
' " is the life of a woman ;" but of all the lives
' of literary women which I have studied, that
' of L. E. L. seems to me the most sorrowful.'*

With another woman of letters, less popular
in her own generation than any of the above-
named, but whose intellectual rank was as

* A kindly notice of Mrs. Maclean—written on the announcement of her death, in the 'Athenæum' of Jan. 5, 1839,
was by Chorley's hand.

much higher as her fame is certain to be more enduring—the late Mrs. Somerville—Chorley was on friendly terms during the period of her residence in England. Writing of the family, in January 1836, to his correspondent in Liverpool, he says: "The Somervilles I like very much. She is quite the pattern of what a literary woman should be, with a cheerful and conversable simplicity of manner that would be rather remarkable in any common person—how much more in so distinguished a star-gazer!" Their vocations in life were too widely asunder to bring them much into correspondence; and, with the exception of an occasional note, he has preserved no memorial of her that can be added to this reference.

During the autumns of 1836, 1837, and 1839, he enlarged his acquaintance with contemporary notabilities, both literary and social, by two visits, partly professional and partly recreative, which he paid to Paris. Such additions as he thereby made to his fund of musical treasures and critical experience, may be reserved for notice in a subsequent chapter. The raptures of surprise and enjoyment which a first visit to the metropolis of pleasure invariably excites in the young, are too familiar to bear repetition ;* and I shall confine my extracts from his minutely detailed journals to such particulars as offer any features of novel, or rather historical, interest.

Among the pleasantest acquaintance whom he made on his first, and improved on his second, visit, were the family of the late Duc de Grâmont, whose Duchess was the sister of his friend Count d'Orsay. They were then living in comparative seclusion at Versailles; their strong Legitimist sympathies forbidding them to appear at the court of the *parvenu* monarch (as they called him) who then filled the throne of France. The chivalrous cour-

---

* Chorley's enthusiasm, warm as it was, did not check the critical tendency which was habitual to him. There is a cynical fancy in this observation upon the position of the cemetery at Père-la-Chaise. ' The view thence over Paris is ' superb. Was the site of this cemetery chosen with the same ' view that made the Indian be buried on the summit of a high ' hill that overlooked his favourite hunting-ground ?'

tesy and high-breeding of the whole family greatly impressed Chorley ; and he dilates with the enthusiasm of an artist on the gratification he had received from a visit to the Chateau of Versailles, in company with the Duke and Duchess, whose traditional tastes and memories were so closely intertwined with its history and relics. One little outburst of characteristic spleen to which the Duchess gave vent, at the spectacle of the new *régime* that had displaced the old, is worth chronicling. The Gallery of Louis Quatorze—among the most splendid apartments of the Château— had been recently restored by Louis Philippe, who had added some candelabra to the furniture. ' " Voilà," said my charming conduc- ' tress, in a low voice full of woman's feeling ; ' " *c'est tout papier-mâché. Aujourd'hui nous* ' " *avons un roi de papier-mâché !*" '

A strong contrast to this home of Legitimist *noblesse* was that of the widow of one of Napoleon's Marshals, Madame la Duchesse d'Abrantes, to whom he was introduced by

his old acquaintance, La Guiccioli. 'I cannot
' describe,' he says, 'how I was repelled by
' this woman. Ugly, stout, coarse, mannish,
' with a hoarse voice and loud grimacing laugh.
' . . . . La Guiccioli told me that she
' takes inconceivable quantities of laudanum—
' and she carries it in her face. Madame
' Ancelot was there, the authoress of " Marie,"
' a Count de la Bayère, and many other people.
' The ladies in a demi-toilette, which it would
' take some time to familiarize to my English
' eye ; the men, ill-looking, ill-dressed, and, it
' seemed to me, impolite as well as vociferous.
' What I heard of the talk was not worth
' hearing ; in short, to retain my respect for
' the society of the Empire, I must hope and
' believe that I stumbled upon an unusually
' unhappy specimen of the doings in the
' Chaussée d'Antin.'

Passing over with a mere allusion his
meetings with persons of less note, such as
Madame la Baronne Cuvier, Lord and Lady
Canterbury—with whom he dined, and met
Lord Lyndhurst—the Prince de Moskowa

(Ney), and the Prince Belgiojoso (remarkable
for his musical gifts), I may quote Chorley's
account of his making acquaintance with two
of the leading French *littérateurs* of the period,
Paul de Kock and Alfred de Vigny. In the
course of his second visit to Paris, having left
a note of introduction at de Kock's house, in
the Boulevard St. Martin, the call was shortly
afterwards returned :—' I opened the door, and
' there stood a short, middle-aged man, with
' a very prepossessing countenance, but intel-
' ligent and melancholy rather than gay, very
' thin and longish black hair (he is, indeed,
' all but bald)—a fine forehead, and mild, but
' observant eyes. He was dressed in a black
' pelisse, faced and cuffed with plush. "Je
' "suis Paul de Kock." I was thoroughly
' glad to see him, and welcomed him my best
' in my bad French ; told him of the pleasure
' I had received from his writings, and we had
' some pleasant talk. His character seems to
' me true to the feeling, and simplicity, and
' shrewdness of his novels. I have yet to find
' whether it be true to those looser parts which

' (pity on them !) make so beautiful a series a
' sealed book to English readers in general.
' But, as he spoke with affection of a son ten
' years old (who plays the piano very well), I
' will believe him to be a good father at all
' events. He referred modestly to his books,
' disclaimed the praise usually given to him as
' a writer merely humorous, and seemed pleased
' and touched by my assuring him (which I
' could honestly do) that I found something in
' them far beyond the emptiness of mirth, and
' instanced the " Frère Jacques," and the last
' scenes of " Le Bon Enfant." He asked me
' whether I had read them in translation. I
' said, No : that I thought his humour untrans-
' lateable ; and he seemed also much pleased.
' We spoke of Victor Hugo, whom we agreed
' in placing at the head of his school; of George
' Sand, whom we equally agreed in regarding
' as a hermaphrodite—a " *génie malade* " ... He
' spoke of Count d'Orsay, till tears came into
' his eyes, and asked me whether he was [still]
' a Frenchman ! He spoke of his own manner
' of life pleasantly and well. He has a little

' cabin or cottage in the country, and there
' he goes *pour se distraire* ; is his own mason,
' his own joiner ; and, truly enough, said that a
' literary man has, beyond all his fellows, need
' of pursuits and occupations in which the mind
' can pleasantly unbend itself, and wander away
' from its fevers or its researches. He spoke
' strongly, but not with bitterness, of his critics.
' "They disliked him," he said, "because he
' "belonged to no coterie, and would not do ser-
' "vice for service." How I admired this ! And
' he said that they called him the author of
' cooks, porters, and scullions. "Well," he said,
' " I console myself, and could silence them if I
' "liked, by saying that I am content, so long as
' "these people don't begin to admire the mon-
' "sters and prodigies of human nature." But
' he seemed to feel to the full the comfort of
' knowing that no enemies or evil speakers can
' hinder that which is written to the heart of a
' people finding its answer there. He also
' spoke of the care and attention which his
' theatrical engagements required, as a reason
' for his not leaving Paris often, or to any great

' distance; and we parted, I full of the most
' agreeable impressions.   I have never seen a
' literary man, whom I should better wish to
' have written works I am fond of studying as
' models than M. Paul de Kock.'

Some days afterwards Chorley called upon
his new acquaintance. 'I found him from
' home; but Madame de Kock, from an inner
' room, invited me to go in, and I am not sorry
' to have accepted the invitation, though, I
' hope, from something better than curiosity
' to see a literary man's *ménage* in Paris. First,
' the room was small and low, an *entresol*, I
' think, with a *parquet*, and no carpet; a tea-
' table set out in the midst; a cottage-piano
' in one corner, and beside it a chair full of
' music; on the wall, opposite the fire-place,
' a portrait of M. de Kock's brother, whom
' Madame de Kock, if I remember right, spoke
' of as being connected with the Dutch Govern-
' ment; and an inner cabinet, shelved with
' books, where, I suppose, he sits to write.
' Madame de Kock was busy doing lace-work;
' a very little woman, *un peu déshabillée peut-*

' *être ;* and though with, perhaps, not much of
' the grand lady in her *abord,* full of true and
' honest pride in her husband, speaking of his
' simple tastes with great pleasure ; how fond
' he is of children, how much he hates money
' transactions with his publishers ; that she is
' always obliged to be the *man* of business ; and
' how thoroughly he is fond of the quiet habits
' which have retained him a tenant of his
' modest *ménage* (against her will) for nineteen
' years. She spoke of his unwillingness to
' quit Paris, even for a visit to his brother,
' whose portrait I saw ; and we were getting
' on very pleasantly, when he entered. The
' more I see, the better I like him. He talked
' very interestingly of Paris, of the life of the
' people on the Boulevards and beyond the
' barriers, which he recommended me to see,
' and of the pleasantness of his situation of resi-
' dence. I said, Yes, but that I was sure I
' never could work if I had a house on the
' Boulevards. "Well," said he, "I find phy-
' " siognomies and figures, above all, costumes
' " and groups in the streets, which are to me

' "invaluable." He then charged me with a
' book for M. le Comte d'Orsay, and on my
' begging permission to read it on the way,
' said he would give me one for myself.   It is
' " Gustave;" but why I note this is, as a trait,
' that the book bears as title-page an illustra-
' tion, which I shall tear out ere I bind this;
' and I am sure that neither he nor she
' (whether from greater honesty of mind—
' whether from the lower tone of national taste,
' as regards the gross and the sufferable) found
' anything strange, or wrong, or objectionable.
' In England no author would have printed
' a book with such a picture—not even Byron.
' . . . . And yet, if I have any skill, this
' French novelist is twice the worth of Byron
' as a husband, a father, and a friend.   It is
' odd to make these distinctions.'

It was in his third visit to Paris (paid in
1839) that Chorley made the acquaintance of
Alfred de Vigny, whom he found 'exceedingly
' pleasant, conversable, *tender*, and friendly—
' perhaps in too *pale a tone* for a man.   But
' what right have I ' (he adds in a parenthesis),

' who have all my life been laughed at for
' like paleness, to object to this ?' Their conversation chiefly turned upon French drama; one of de Vigny's remarks on which, Chorley notes as chiming in with his own preconceptions, viz., ' that the Oromanes and ' Coriolanus of Corneille and Voltaire were ' *words*, not *characters*, as distinguished from ' the beings of Shakspeare.' On another occasion they talked of Molière, whom de Vigny defended ' against the charge of want of en-' thusiasm and passion sometimes brought ' against him; averring that the passion of ' " Le Misanthrope " " was none the less pas-' " sion for its being hooped, petticoated, and ' " wigged." ' In de Vigny's company Chorley went, for the first time, to see Rachel's performance in Voltaire's " Tancrède." Though ' very much struck with the remarkable force ' and emphasis of her declamation, and the ' propriety of her by-play,' he thought her deficient in action, and her attitudes too ' constantly in *ordonnance*, as though the ' *pose*, having been once found effective, was

' repeated whenever invention fell short.'
Her acting on a subsequent occasion as
Camille, in Corneille's ' Horace,' materially
altered his estimate of her. ' It is a great
' triumph, and I am converted to her. . . . .
' In that wonderful scene with the soldier
' she was sublime: the quivering play of
' her hands, every fibre listening and yield-
' ing and struggling with despair, as one
' who would deal with it herself, and let it
' have its way with others; the sinking form,
' the horror-stricken countenance, were all
' in the best style of art; to me finer and
' more affecting than her tremendous taunts
' to her brother, every word of which was
' a heart-string broken, and a drop of heart's
' blood shed against him, to pile on his head
' " the mountain of her curse." '

On another occasion he was present at a
performance by the great actress Mars, then
in the golden sunset of her powers and fame.
' The piece was " Marie." To be sure, in the
' epoch of girlhood her physical powers would
' not second her conception; but as the young

' wife of the *financier*, all dressed out in
' diamonds and flowers, and trying to
' smother an old passion under the semblance
' of gaiety and worldliness, she was admir-
' able. One speech, the great speech wherein,
' on her old lover reproaching her with
' coldness, she turns and tells him of the
' agonies she has endured, the death that is
' in her heart, was more the language of
' anguish than anything I ever heard.
' Then what could exceed her acting in
' the last act, when, having thought all her
' trials were on the point of being rewarded,
' and looking forward to the future with a calm
' happiness, not so wholly meditative, as to
' show that all capacity for enjoyment is dead
' within her, she finds that her lover has trans-
' ferred his affections—to her daughter! That
' charming, exquisite, girlish little Anais in the
' part of the daughter! with a beauty, a fresh-
' ness, and a bird-like gaiety! No : we have
' nothing like it in England!'

On returning from Paris, after his second
visit, in the winter of 1837, Chorley cour-

teously undertook the escort of a lady known to him as the mother of an old acquaintance, Mr. Henry Reeve, distinguished in official life as registrar of the Privy Council, and in literature as editor of the ' Edinburgh Review,' and the translator of ' De Tocqueville.' Early in the following year, his acquaintance with Mr. Reeve having ripened into friendship, they entered into an arrangement to keep house together. They took some "luxuriously comfortable lodgings," as Chorley describes them, in Chapel Street, Grosvenor Place, where their bachelor-partnership continued until Mr. Reeve's marriage in December, 1841. During these years Chorley mixed a good deal in London society, and, in company with his " house-mate," entertained freely. The *réunions* which they gathered, thanks to Mr. Reeve's extensive acquaintance, were more than ordinarily brilliant; and the musical part of the entertainment was always of the highest excellence, owing to Chorley's intimacy with the musical world. Mendelssohn, Moscheles, Liszt, Ernst,

David, Batta, and almost all the great instrumentalists of the day performed there at various times. Among the guests whose names Chorley has recorded were Mr. Carlyle, Mr. and Mrs. Procter, Mr. Kenyon, Mr. and Mrs. Somerville, Mr. and Mrs. Basil Montagu, Harness, Poley the German Orientalist, Count Montalembert, M. Rio, Westmacott, Doyle (H.B.), Mr. Milnes (Lord Houghton), Mr. and Mrs. Austin, Mrs. Jameson, Miss Martineau, and Miss Sedgwick, the American authoress. A visit of some duration was paid to them by M. Léon Faucher, the eminent Parisian journalist, and his wife, at the time of Her Majesty's coronation.

Of a curious incident that occurred during the period of his housekeeping with Mr. Reeve, in connection with an episode of adventure in a chequered career which has but lately closed, Chorley has left a brief reminiscence. The late Emperor of the French, then Prince Louis Napoleon Bonaparte, was at that time residing in England, after the failure of his expedition to Strasburg. ' He was con-

' tent,' as Chorley says of him, ' to figure as a
' lion in the circles of the Mrs. Leo Hunters
' of his time, who cared not what manner of
' curiosities they drew together, patriots, poets,
' military men, barristers, acquitted criminals,
' most of all, political refugees, or, as a friend
' of mine once humorously described them,
' " Charity Poles." ' In these circles, and as a
frequent guest at Gore House, Chorley had
made his acquaintance, and entertained a
different opinion of his abilities from that
formed by superficial observers, who accounted
his taciturnity an evidence of stupidity. ' He
' used to drive me frequently from Kensington
' to Hyde Park Corner, when we left Gore
' House, and would make shrewd remarks, and
' ask searching questions about subjects con-
' cerning which he desired to have informa-
' tion. . . . Mr. Reeve—whose keen interest
' and close participation in matters concerning
' foreign politics is no secret—was then in
' constant relation with M. Guizot, the French
' ambassador in London. . . . It was on the
' Saturday before the Prince's attempt was

' made at Boulogne, that my house-mate,
' before going out for the day, left with me a
' note to be taken by our joint servant to the
' French embassy in Manchester Square. The
' servant. aforesaid, Jonathan . . . . was a
' rough talkative man, not a little vain . . . .
' of the notoriety of some among our habitual
' guests. While I was dressing for dinner, he
' began to tell me that, during his evening
' rounds, he had seen in the Mall in St. James's
' Park two carriages duly appointed, and to
' them came alone from Carlton Gardens, where
' Prince Louis was then residing, himself, his
' faithful friend, Count Persigny, and one or
' two other gentlemen. Jonathan had stayed
' to gossip with some of the servants, to whom
' he was well known, and brought, on their
' authority, the news that Prince Louis " was
' going to France to kick up a row." Treating
' the matter (who would not have done so ?)
' as a piece of pure fiction, and averse to
' anything like scandal proceeding from our
' house, especially in the case of one so deli-
' cately circumstanced as Prince Louis, I spoke·

' angrily to the man, and charged him on no
' account to repeat the absurd tale, least of all
' at the French embassy, to which he was
' going that same evening with a note from
' Reeve. This he promised to do, and kept
' his promise. My dinner that day was at
' Gore House, *tête-à-tête* with Lady Bles-
' sington. When we were alone at dessert,
' our talk ran on English servants, and the
' liberties too frequently taken by them with
' the names of their masters and their masters'
' friends. I mentioned what had passed at
' home, as an instance. She treated the tale
' as I had done. " Why," she said, " I drove
' " down to Carlton Gardens only yesterday
' " to leave a parcel there, which Prince Louis
' " had undertaken to send for me to Paris by
' " Prince Baiocchi ; he came out and spoke to
' " me." We passed on to something else.
' When I went home, I told the thing to
' Reeve, as a good story. After I had left
' Gore House, Lady Blessington told the
' same to Count d'Orsay, who got home late,
' also as an absurdity. Reeve went, according

' to his note, to breakfast with M. Guizot
' on the Sunday morning, and, of course, did
' not trouble the grave man in office with
' such a piece of nonsense. Monday passed,
' and Tuesday ; on Wednesday afternoon late,
' some one rode up to the carriage of Lady
' Blessington, who was driving in the park,
' open-mouthed with the news of the attempt
' at Boulogne, and the arrest of the pre-
' tender to the French throne. " Good God!
' " to be sure," she cried, in her eager way,
' " know all about it; Chorley told me on
' " Saturday!"

' I have often speculated on the "ifs" and
' "ands" which might have happened, had we
' all four not disregarded the affair as a prepos-
' terous tale, and had M. Guizot been apprised
' on the Sunday morning. There have been
' days in which we might have been all ac-
' cused, and with a fair show of circumstan-
' tial evidence, of complicity in the treason.

' During the time when Prince Louis was
' imprisoned in Ham, by the failure of his
' attempt, covered with ridicule, I was in

' occasional communication with him, with
' the view of beguiling his hours of captivity,
' and heard of him constantly—from him,
' more than once. When his " Idées Napo-
' léoniennes," written in his dungeon, were
' to be published by Colburn, I was invited,
' with his concurrence, to translate the book
' into English; and a set of proofs, corrected
' by himself, was sent me. I did not accept
' the task, mainly because I have never put
' my hand to a task of the kind, without
' some special knowledge of that which I
' professed to handle. For the same reason,
' whatever have been my prejudices or pre-
' dilections, on yet stronger grounds, I would
' never take service as a political journalist;
' such subjects are too grave ones to be under-
' taken merely as the means of gaining a
' livelihood. Whether right or wrong, I kept
' the proofs of the book by me for a long
' time, and was very near being brought into
' trouble by them, as under.

   ' I was going into France, before the Prince
' escaped from Ham, and while making the

' hasty provisions for my journey, totally
' overlooked the fact that my writing-book
' contained some of the sheets of this perilous
' production, annotated by the writer. For-
' tunately, the *douanier* at Calais knew my
' face, and did not open my bundle of travel-
' ling wares. I destroyed the proofs, not con-
' ceiving that one day they might become a
' literary curiosity, no matter what was the
' intrinsic poorness of the work.

' When Prince Louis made his escape from
' Ham, I was one of the first persons whom
' he called on; and it seems as if it were but
' yesterday that he told me, from one of my
' easy-chairs, the particulars of the manner of
' his deliverance, too well known to the world
' for the tale to be told again here. To the
' last days of his residence in England, he
' continued to show a recollection of the very
' trifling services I could render him, such as
' has not been the rule with others on an
' equality with myself, to whom chance has
' enabled me to give important assistance at
' critical junctures of their lives.'

This chapter must conclude with a few
brief notices of other lions of London society
whom Chorley was so fortunate as to meet
during these years. Under date of 15th March,
1838, he chronicles his meeting, at a *soirée*
given by Miss Martineau, with the two Misses
Berry :—' Horace Walpole's Miss Berrys.
' What luck to have met with them!   They
' are more like one's notion of ancient French-
' women than anything I have ever seen;
' rouged, with the remains of some beauty,
' managing large fans like the Flirtillas, &c.,
' &c. of Ranelagh, and besetting Macready
' . . . . about the womanly proprieties of
' the character of Pauline in the " Lady of
' " Lyons," till one thought of the *Critique de
' l'Ecole des Femmes*. It is not often that
' I have heard anything so brilliant and
' amusing.'   Of these ladies, ' women of the
' world, women of refinement, women of lite-
' rary dilettantism,' as they were, ' one of
' whom made a good appearance in author-
' ship by her " Comparative View of English
' " and French Society during the Revolution "

' —who kept open house in London, fre-
' quented by the choicest literary people,
' during some thirty years ' — he recounts
a singular instance of literary ignorance :
' When that most charming of modern
' antique books, Landor's " Pericles and
' " Aspasia," appeared, subsequently to his
' " Gebir," his " Imaginary Conversations,"
' and even (I think) his " Examination of
' " Shakspeare," on his name being passed
' round in their circle by some enterprising
' guest, Miss Berry said — " Mr. Landor ?
' What has he written ?" '

A few days after this meeting, he was asked
' to breakfast at Mr. Kenyon's, to meet Dr.
' Southey, and Mr. Ticknor, of Boston, who
' seemed a gentleman and a man of letters at
' once. I never met any literary man who
' so thoroughly answered my expectations as
' Southey. His face is at once shrewd, thought-
' ful, and quick, if not irritable, in its expres-
' sion ; a singular deficiency of space in its
' lower portion, but no deficiency of feature
' or expression ; his manner cold, but still ; in

' conversation, bland and gentle, and not
' nearly so dogmatic as his writings would
' lead one to imagine. Talking, and talking
' well, a good deal about America. . . .
' He was speaking of Miss Martineau patiently,
' but without respect, describing her as " talk-
' " ing more glibly than any woman he had
' " ever seen, and with such a notion of her
' " own infallibility." I was more agreeably
' impressed by Southey than I have, for a
' long time, been by any stranger.'

On another occasion he dined at the Dilkes'
to meet Hood—' as quaint, as lazy, as deaf as
' ever ; but always one of the most original
' people in his drolleries I ever met. There is
' a certain indescribable oddity that amuses me
' more than I can well express. Generally,
' funny people are detestable.' Among the
lions of this calibre, whom he seems to have
specially disliked, was the late James Smith,
one of the authors of the " Rejected Addresses ;" chiefly, perhaps, on account of
' his Garrick Club talk,' and the trick of
' whistling the airs of his odious comic songs '

during a theatrical performance. He was not
more favourably impressed by Haynes Bayly,
whom, with his wife, he met at a fancy
ball, in the summer of 1838. There is a lu-
dicrous *vraisemblance* about his sketch of their
appearance: ' Till I saw them, I never under-
' stood the full force of the reproach of *Bath*
' *fashion;* tawdry, airy, sentimental, vulgar;
' he with a pen-and-red-ink complexion, and a
' hyacinthine Romeo wig, dancing, and be-
' having prettily to all the little girls in the
' room; she in an old French dress, rouged,
' *fade*, haggard: what a pair of shabby old
' butterflies !'*

Miss Sedgwick, the American authoress,
who visited England in 1839, met with a
more flattering portrait from his pen : ' She
' is decidedly the pleasantest American woman
' I have ever seen, with more of a turn for
' humour, and less American sectarianism.
' The twang, to be sure, there is in plenty;

---

* That there is no malice in this portrait of a fellow crafts-
man's *personnel* may be seen from Chorley's generous estimate
of him in an obituary notice (' Athenæum,' May 4th, 1839).

' and the toilette is the dowdiness (not the
' finery) of the backwoods; but then she is
' lively, kind, heart-warm; and I feel, some-
' how or other, almost on friendly terms with
' her, though I never spoke more than twenty
' consecutive words to her.'

These candid, and often caustic, sketches of
character and manners, it must be remembered, are extracts from a journal of which
the publication was never contemplated; nor
should this now be given to them if any to
whom they might occasion pain were presumed
to be living. Chorley himself was far too kindly
and sensitive to have perpetrated what he was
the first to reprobate in others, the impertinence and cruelty of literary vivisection.   In
a letter to his Liverpool correspondent, dated
August 1st, 1841, he thus notices a recent
breach of this canon of good taste, by the lady
who had produced so agreeable an impression
upon him when they met a year or two before :—

"Miss Sedgwick * has been returning the

* In a volume of 'Letters.'

compliment of all English journalists, by putting us all round on paper, to a degree which is too bad. She asked, it seems, poor dear Miss Mitford's servants what wages they received, and the like; and, I hear, has written that which is likely most sadly to compromise some of the Italian refugees in America, who were negotiating with the Austrian Government for a restoration to their families. I liked her so well in private, as an honest-minded, simple-mannered, cultivated woman, that I am really more vexed than there is any occasion for. I fear the next cage of Transatlantic birds will not run much chance of being very liberally dinnered and soiréed here; only everything passes off like a nine-days' wonder!"

CHAPTER VI.

Progress and experiences as a musical critic between 1834 and 1841—Original gifts and acquirements—Persistence of principle—Conservatism in theory—Development of taste—Illustrative extracts from journals—Visits to France in 1836, 1837, and 1839 — Interview with Chopin—Acquaintance with systems of Wilhem and Mainzer—National singing-schools in England—Tours in Germany, 1839, 1840, 1841—Intimacy with, and letters from, Mendelssohn—Journey in company with him and Moscheles—Stay at Leipsic—Anecdotes of Mendelssohn—Schumann—Sonnet to Mendelssohn's son—Subsequent letters—Publication of " Music and Manners," &c.

WHAT original qualifications Chorley possessed for the profession of musical criticism I have little means of determining, beyond the allusions that he himself makes to the subject in the autobiographical chapters with which this memoir opens. That he was gifted with a singularly acute ear and retentive memory;

that, thanks to his Liverpool teachers, his passionate love of the art was based upon a sound knowledge of the science of music; and that he had acquired a familiarity with the works of its greatest masters that was wide if not profound, are facts about which there can be no dispute. To one thus endowed and informed, a regular course of attendance during several months of the year at the choicest performances of sacred and secular music in London, must of itself have constituted a professional education of no ordinary value. The task of habitually estimating in an organ of credit and influence the achievements of ministers of the art so great as those who were then before the public—of Rossini, Mendelssohn, and Meyerbeer, Paganini, Liszt, Thalberg and Ernst, Pasta, Malibran, Grisi, Schroeder-Devrient, Adelaide Kemble, Donzelli, Rubini, Lablache, Tamburini; and of pronouncing upon the fate of those who aspired to stand beside them, must, to one so ambitious and conscientious as Chorley, have operated as a stimulus, stronger than any

other that could have been devised, to acquit
himself worthily of his trust, and make up, by
increased accuracy of observation and impartiality of judgment, for any defects in his
early training. It is evident that he quickly
impressed his employers with a sense of his
fitness, as within a year after his connection
with the ' Athenæum ' he seems to have been
entrusted with the direction of its musical
department; and thenceforth the notices of
opera and concert performances, together with
the reviews of new music, continued to be
written by him almost exclusively, down to
the year 1868. To follow with anything
like accuracy the indications of a gradual
maturing of taste and modification of opinion,
which are doubtless to be found in a series of
critical estimates extending over so long a
period, would be possible only to an educated
musician. Such evidence of intellectual growth
as is patent to the eye of an unskilled observer
like myself, must not pass without notice,
more especially as side by side with it there
is apparent that persistence of *principle* which

is characteristic of all sincere and earnest natures, the granite foundation of conviction which underlies and outlasts all shifting sands of opinion. To this, as of right, attention must be first directed.

To eulogise an art-journalist of our own day for conspicuous integrity in the exercise of his calling might seem either to "damn him with faint praise," or cast an undeserved slur upon the general body of the profession. But it would be affectation to assume that thirty or forty years ago the critical press, either of this country or the Continent, occupied the same honourable position in public estimation that it occupies now, or to ignore the discredit of venality and sycophancy which then attached to organs of wide circulation and influence. To what extent suspicion was really justified is a question which cannot be discussed here, but one illustration in point may be noticed in passing. All who are acquainted with operatic history will be likely to remember how—less than thirty years ago— a sinking manager contrived for a while to float the wreck of his fortune, and tide over a season of failure, by invoking the aid of a clique of journalists, whose mission it was to stimulate public curiosity into feverish excitement, by alternately announcing the advent, and apologising for the delay, of an unparagoned singer whose success was to retrieve all past disappointments and inaugurate a new era of glory. The caustic narrative of that episode which Chorley, who had waged a ceaseless opposition against the cabal in question, has put on record in his " Thirty Years' Musical Recollections,"* may be referred to by those who have forgotten the circumstances.

More than one scene in which he was an actor furnishes proof that, on the score of uprightness and clean-handedness, his professional career was sufficiently exceptional to justify special comment. No stress can be laid upon ordinary instances of solicitation. Every journalist, whose verdict is worth a bribe, has doubtless been insulted by attempts, more or

* Vol. i. pp. 271—274.

less transparent, to influence his judgment in a given direction. In the majority of cases, such attempts are made by ignorant and ill-bred persons on behalf of themselves or their friends; and nothing more can fairly be inferred than the folly or baseness of the individuals concerned. Chorley has noted two or three such instances in his experience which I do not consider worthy of insertion here, because, however curious in themselves, they are insufficient to warrant a general inference. But the following illustration has a far wider bearing. The individual concerned was a foreign composer of eminent genius and reputation, to whose works Chorley had long rendered his tribute of admiration, as spontaneous as it was well-merited, but whom he had never met. On the first occasion of the *maestro's* coming to England, writes Chorley, in his narrative of the incident, ' I paid him a visit, ' anxious to offer him such attention as lay in ' my power, by way of testifying my gratitude ' in private, as I had again and again done in ' print, for the rare pleasure he had afforded

' me. In a few days my visit was returned
' with every sign of courtesy. But when my
' caller rose to take his leave, I perceived a cer-
' tain unmistakable thing—a *rouleau*—drawn
' from his pocket, and within an inch of my
' table. There was nothing to do but to close
' his hand over it, with a gesture towards the
' place from which it had been extracted. I
' see, while I write, his look of unfeigned
' astonishment as I said (to avoid misunder-
' standing), "It is not our English habit."
' What makes the matter more curious still, is
' that some years later I heard the story [of
' my refusing this offer] told in Paris in a
' company of artists as something *peculiar*—no
' person being aware that one of the two
' parties concerned was present.' It is inconceivable that a man of such intellectual rank
and good breeding as the composer in question
would have ventured to compromise his reputation in the way described, unless his experience of artistic journalism had convinced
him that "every man had his price." The
surprise which the discovery of his mistake

occasioned, not only to himself but to the circle of *confrères* to whom he must have communicated it, puts the exceptional nature of the occurrence beyond the reach of doubt.

This, as will be hereafter seen, was by no means an isolated experience in Chorley's professional life, but it is assuredly not upon the strength of a hundred such instances—for which he would have been ashamed to take or receive credit—that I am desirous of resting his claim to be considered *sans peur et sans reproche.* The whole tenor of his critical career, so far as I have been able to follow it, seems pervaded and consecrated by a single aim. That Art should be true to herself, her purpose high, her practice stainless, was a creed which he never wearied of preaching. Against any tradition of the past, or innovation of the present, that savoured of falsehood or trick; against all pretenders, who concealed their nakedness by meretricious display or arrogant self-assertion, he ceaselessly protested and inveighed. Alike to the bribery of managers, the venality of journalists and *claqueurs*, the extravagant assumption of composers, and the insolent vanity of singers and instrumentalists, he showed himself a bitter, almost a remorseless, enemy. His persistence brought him many enemies in return, but they never made him swerve or keep silence. The tenacity with which he maintained his ground upon all questions connected with the ethics of art and literature— such as the impartiality of journalism, the responsibilities of *artistes* to managers, and of both to the public, the tactics employed to advertise the " Music of the Future," and the like—has often struck me as a remarkable instance of mental " atavism." Dormant, to all appearance, in the intervening generations, this quality seems directly traceable to those sturdy Recusant ancestors of his who, during two centuries, were content to be mulcted and spoiled by Tudor, Stuart, and Guelph, rather than surrender the faith which they eventually sealed upon the scaffold. Invidious as the possession of such firmness often is to a man in life, it insensibly exerts an influence that is at last appreciably felt, extorts the admiration even of his enemies, and stands out prominently in his character when he is dead. Freely as the epithets of " obstinate " and " crotchetty " have been applied to Chorley by those who loved him—epithets intensified a hundredfold by those who hated him—I doubt if any will now be found to dispute the justice of the emphatic ascription of " honesty," rendered to him in my hearing by a brother critic who attended his funeral; or dissent from the verdict of the leading evening journal when it announced his death,—that " by the bold and courageous character of his writing, and his integrity of purpose, he exercised great influence upon the state and progress of music in this country."*

When looking back, through a vista of thirty years, upon his professional life, and comparing his matured impressions (drawn from recollection alone) of the *artistes* he had heard, with the critical estimates he had pro-

Pall Mall Gazette,' Feb. 16, 1872.

nounced upon them at the time, Chorley
could say that he 'had found no discrepancy
'betwixt past and present judgments wòrth
'adverting to.'   (Introduction to "Thirty
Years' Musical Recollections," p. xi.)   Although this statement must not be taken *au
pied de la lettre*, it no doubt expresses with
sufficient accuracy the gross result of the
comparison in question, and may be applied
even more widely to characterise the rapidity
and accuracy with which he arrived at his
conclusions, and the conservative tone of his
criticism generally.   He doubtless owed the
first of these characteristics, in great measure,
to an exceptional development of natural
faculty, to which experience gave increased
strength and fineness.   His extreme sensibility of ear* enabled him to seize at a single

---

* It was naturally acute rather than accurate, as he
testified in his Lectures on National Music (1862). 'I have
'met no one with quicker and more exact and retentive
'power than myself; and it has been in incessant exercise
'during thirty years; but not a few of these had elapsed before
'I discovered that I habitually heard every musical sound
'*half a note too sharp*, and this without respect to the pitch

hearing, and his singularly retentive memory to produce for subsequent reflection, the salient features of a musical composition, which an ordinarily gifted hearer would only succeed in grasping after repeated attendances and hours of quiet study. His journals attest that this promptness of apprehension, in a rudimentary state, was possessed by him almost from the first. Their records of musical experiences, which date from 1832, are repeatedly interspersed with *motivi*, scored from memory, but quoted with as much facility as if they had been verses from a favourite poet. Some of these passages were, no doubt, familiar to him, but others were avowedly transcribed after hearing them for the first time. Several such instances could be cited from the journals of his visits to France and Germany in 1839 and 1840; and the evidence of his faculty was remarkable enough to excite the surprise even of

---

' to which the instrument or the voice was tuned. It took
' me no small time and pains to verify this fact. . . . . Now
' everything I hear passes through the process of translation.'

Mendelssohn (*vide* p. 317, *post*). This advantage of acquiring rapidly and retaining surely the material upon which his judgment was to be exercised, would of itself account for the decisive tone of his enunciations; but there can be no doubt that it received substantial weight and justification from the careful thought which he had originally given to the theory and practice of music. There is reason, moreover, to believe that the artistic canons to which his mind had subscribed when it first devoted itself to their definition were those which the judgment of his maturer years deliberately confirmed. I am not aware that any signal instance of inconsistency, akin to that which has so often bewildered the disciples of a contemporary teacher in the sister art of painting, has ever been proved against Chorley. As an illustration of his persistent adherence to a theory which he had once adopted as true, I may notice that in a lecture which he delivered at the Royal Institution in 1861, upon the relations of poetry and music, he elaborated

the same principles already adverted to as
laid down by him in a critique of Moore's
"Irish Melodies" in the 'Athenæum' of
1834. In later life this natural bias of his
mind to conservatism displayed itself still
more prominently, and exposed him, with
some show of reason, to the imputation of
dogmatism and finality, but it never rendered
him insensible to the impression of new ideas.
His apprehension was never more happily
manifested than in the promptness with
which he discerned the signs that herald
the sudden advent of genius, nor his persistence more worthily employed than in the
unwearied pertinacity with which he urged
upon public attention the claims of any
whose recognition was too long delayed.
An illustration of the one, in connection
with the name of Mr. Arthur Sullivan; of the
other, in connection with that of M. Gounod,
will not fail to occur to all readers of the
' Athenæum.'

Chorley's own statement above quoted as
to the absence of discrepancy between his

earlier and later judgments, must not, as I have said, be taken quite literally, or without due limitation. It should rather be interpreted in the general sense already explained, and practically restricted to cases where the evidence was sufficiently complete to enable him to arrive at a decision at once. It would cause an entirely erroneous impression, if taken to mean that his mind was never in suspense, nor subject to those tentative fluctuations of opinion which every mind must undergo that has not been prematurely stunted, or warped by prejudice. His early estimates of singers like Grisi and Pasta assuredly differed from his later judgments, in so far as the glowing rapture of a young enthusiast differs from the discriminating enjoyment of a middle-aged *habitué*: the fascination to which he yielded when the vigour and richness of such music as Meyerbeer's impressed him for the first time, was moderated by the subsequent discovery of deficiencies which impaired their value.

With respect to Grisi, for example—whose

glorious endowments as an actress and singer
were, in the opinion of some of her ad-
mirers, too imperfectly recognised and grudgingly praised by him in his later criticisms
—a gradual subsidence of enthusiasm and
modification of judgment are clearly apparent.
The outburst of rapture with which he
chronicles, in April 1834, his first impressions of her performance in "La Gazza
Ladra," would satisfy the demands of her
most *exigeant* worshipper. 'I can neither be
' cool nor critical over this dear creature.
' Her voice is deliciously pure and young, and
' she sings as if she loved her art, and had its
' resources at her feet ; still I don't think that
' she has by any means reached the zenith of
' her powers. Her execution is brilliant and
' fearless—sometimes a little too florid—her
' arms like sculpture, but used in a thousand
' ways which would make any sculptor's
' fortune ; her hair magnificent, her action
' easy, passionate, and never extravagant;
' some of the bursts of feeling, the " *Ben chè*
' " *io sola* " in " La Gazza," and in her trial

' scene, and in the *coda* of the funeral march,
' were positively electrifying, and made tears
' come in harder eyes than mine. . . . She
' must play Desdemona—she is the woman of
' women for the part! In " Anna Bolena "
' I felt where Pasta's low-veiled tones were
' wanting, and the piece is so dreary that she
' produced less effect than in " La Gazza." . . .
' Still, her playing in the last scene was
' splendid, and recalled to one Miss Mitford's
' most expressive personation of

 ' " Bright chattering Madness, and sedate Despair."

' I have dared to say that I prefer her to
' Malibran, and wait her Donna Anna with
' some anxiety, to see whether I shall be
' allowed by my conscience to let such a
' record stand.' Later in the same year he
pronounces her ' perfect ' in " Donna Anna ;"
her ' first scene could not be surpassed '—
her singing in " Semiramide " as ' all brightness and power ;' her voice throwing out its
' glorious *altissimo* notes in positive floods
' of brilliancy and power ;' her acting in

"Otello" as 'magnificent,' and in "Anna Bolena" as 'sublime.' In May, 1837, his verdict is that she is 'more superb than 'ever,' but the warmth of these epithets soon suffers a gradual *diminuendo*. In his journal of August, 1839, there occurs such an entry as this: 'Grisi (in "Norma") singing false, 'and certainly falling off;' and in the 'Athenæum' of May, 1840, she is described as 'still something too abrupt and emphatic 'for our "Desdemona."' Further modifications are apparent in later notices, and the resulting average of these alternations of praise and censure is embodied in his deliberate estimate of her in the "Musical Recollections," vol. i. pp. 108–117. Other instances to the same effect could be readily adduced.

How just in the main were his contemporary verdicts, how accurate his forecasts have proved to be, has been repeatedly observed since his death. That his judgment was occasionally at fault is undeniable, and, with a candour too rare among critics, he was

the first to call attention to the failure. An
instance in point may be cited from the
musical annals of 1844–6. On the appointment of Signor (now Sir Michael) Costa, in
the former year, as conductor of the Philharmonic Society's Concerts, Chorley denounced
it as strange and unsuitable, prophesying
that 'the only result of such proceeding
' would inevitably be outrageously unpopular.'
('Athenæum,' 1844, p. 1051). He was
made sensible of his error after hearing the
first concert under the new *régime,* and
hastened to retract. ' Without unnecessary
' words of exaggeration, it may be stated as
' past question that the first Philharmonic
' Concert established Signor Costa in the
' foremost rank of conductors of classical
' music, and justified the directors in their
' choice. As we somewhat mistrusted the
' discretion of his appointment, it behoves us
' emphatically to say that we have heard no
' Philharmonic performance to compare with
' Monday's (March 16th). The orchestra is
' entirely under the control of Signor Costa's

' *bâton*,' &c. (' Athenæum,' 1846, p. 298). I
am indebted for this illustration to a recently
published volume of " Musical Recollections,"
by an accomplished connoisseur, which bears
testimony, doubly valuable by reason of
its independence, to the general sagacity of
Chorley's criticism, by the copious reference it
makes to them as the utterances of a high
authority.*

Chorley's own volume of recollections already cited furnishes a *résumé* of his experiences and opinions in musical matters, so
much more completely and accurately than
they could otherwise be supplied, that I shall
not attempt to supplement it. It may enhance
the value of this volume, however, in the
eyes of those who have read it without knowing anything of the writer, if I say a few
words which Chorley could not say for himself,
respecting the means by which he obtained
his experience and informed his judgment.

* " Musical Recollections of the Last Half-century "
(Tinsley, 1872). *Vide* Preface, p. ix. vol. ii. pp. 41–42, and
passim.

All lovers of music and frequenters of its public performance in London during the last · forty years, whether of opera, oratorio, or concert, will probably be familiar with his figure; but only his intimates will be likely to know how ubiquitous he really was, and what toil and cost he was ready to expend in the discharge of his duty. Year after year, from 1836 to 1868, and often more than once a year, he was in the habit of making expeditions to the Continent, for the purpose of hearing music that could not be heard, or seeing *artistes* who would not perform in England. In spite of his weak *physique* he would undertake these expeditions at any season, and sometimes at a moment's warning. Long night-journeys in the most pitiless of weather and unaccommodating of conveyances, interruptions of pre-arranged plans of travel and needful seasons of repose, were cheerfully submittedto if Music were the siren that summoned him. His Continental journals abound with evidences of a vagrancy that any one unacquainted with his motive would naturally ascribe to the restlessness of disease. Having settled down, to all appearance, for a week at Leipsic, he suddenly emerges at Berlin, lured by the report of a performance of Gluck. From Dresden he hurries off to Paris on a similar errand; or, when bound for the South, diverges from his route for miles to be present at a concert which Liszt has announced at Mayence. Whenever he was able so to time his annual holiday as to attend these performances in the course of it, his professional and personal expenditure was always duly adjusted.*

The visits which he paid to France in 1836, 1837, and 1839, and to Germany in 1839, 1840, and 1841, were more memorable to him, perhaps, than any other, both as enlarging the sphere of his experience and reputation, and giving rise to the formation of one of his

---

* It deserves to be recorded, to the credit alike of employer and employed, that the late Sir Wentworth Dilke entertained so high an opinion of Chorley's scrupulous honour, that he instructed his publisher (Mr. Francis) to pay whatever sums were submitted as expenses on such occasions, without asking for any explanation.

most cherished friendships. In Paris he became familiar with music of Meyerbeer, Auber, Halévy, and Chopin, then and for some time afterwards little known or regarded in London, and added the two last composers to the number of his acquaintance At his interview with Chopin, whom he describes 'as 'pale, thin, and profoundly melancholy' in appearance, he was gratified by hearing the composer perform a succession of characteristic *morceaux* on the piano. 'His touch,' writes Chorley, 'has all the delicacy of a 'woman's, but is not so fine. *Voilà* a very 'impalpable distinction! but a distinction for 'all that. I mean to say that I don't think 'any female finger of so small a *timbre* would 'have produced a tone in its weight so sig-'nificant without the slightest impression of 'pressure. The long extensions with which 'his music abounds, again, are managed by 'throwing the whole hand forwards in a 'manner which I can hardly fancy a woman 'doing without making a jerk. In the first 'example I was struck by the delicacy, almost

' *ad libitum,* of the *fiorimenti* he introduced—
' all the harmonies are helped and massed to-
' gether by the aid of the pedal. . . . .
' No want of fire and passion, no want of neat-
' ness, if you regard the whole thing as *veiled*
' *music,* and such it is.'

Nourrit, Duprez and Mario, Persiani, Pau-line Garcia, Dorus-Gras, Cinti-Damoreau, Nau, and Anna Thillon, were among the eminent singers whom Chorley heard for the first time in Paris. Here, too, he familiarised himself with the methods of instruction in part-singing then recently introduced by Mainzer and Wilhem. Of the latter he entertained a high opinion, and on his return home lent all his influence in support of Mr. Hullah's efforts to establish a similar system in this country.

The chief feature of his earliest visit to Germany in 1839 was the introduction to Mendelssohn, which laid the foundation of their friendship. No contemporary composer occupied a higher place in his estimation; and his praise, both in public and private, had

not been stinted. After hearing the performance of " St. Paul," at Exeter Hall, in September 1837, he writes in his journal : ' As
' music this ranks high—next to Handel's—
' so much simpler and less cloyingly enriched
' than Spohr's. . . . Deliciously *cantabile*
' for the voices—in places very grand—in
' places fanciful without eccentricity ; and al-
' ways beautifully expressive. Mendelssohn is
' certainly *the* Oratorio-writer.'

The detailed notice in the ' Athenæum,' of
which this is the rough draft, and other
expressions of his critical admiration had
probably been brought to the composer's
notice by their common friend Moscheles.
Chorley's visit to the Brunswick Festival, in
1839, was, at all events, expected by Mendelssohn, and they met as old acquaintance. The
cicumstances of their meeting, among other
memorabilia of his musical experience on the
Continent during this and the two following
years, Chorley has sufficiently described in his
" Music and Manners in France and Germany." That volume is mainly compiled from

the elaborate journals which he kept on the occasion; but a few notes which, for obvious reasons, he omitted to transcribe from them may now without impropriety be added to supplement it. The first impression made upon him by Mendelssohn's appearance is thus described :—

' I had already made myself aware that he ' was not in the least like any portrait I have ' seen, and that he is a capital conductor, ' though in quite a different *genre* from Mos- ' cheles—as different as their two musics. . . . ' He is very handsome, with a particularly ' sweet laugh, and a slight cloud (not to call ' it thickness) upon his utterance, which ' seemed like the voice of some friend. . . . ' Nothing could be kinder than he was.'

A few days later there is an entry in the journal which describes Mendelssohn's power as a pianist : ' He played his own Concerto ' (in D) on a peculiarly ungrateful Vienna ' pianoforte ; but no matter. It is thoroughly ' artistic playing ; a certain organ-fullness, ' but not organ-heaviness, in his touch ; a

' capital management of time—so free, and still
' so not too free ; a complete freedom from all
' possible mannerism ; a fullness of expression
' without the least constraint ; a complete ab-
' sence of all *petitesse* ; and a degree of ani-
' mating spirit communicating itself to his
' orchestra, the mixture of which seems to
' make him as essential to his own music as is
' Thalberg.'*

Their converse was thoroughly cordial
during this visit, and they frankly inter-
changed ideas and discussed joint projects,
which are referred to in the subjoined letters †
of Mendelssohn, written after Chorley's return
to England. Of his own letters, to which
these are replies, I have found no copies.

"Leipzig, 28th Feb., 1840.

"MY DEAR FRIEND.

"Your letter gave me a very great
pleasure. I wish your occupations might

* For a more elaborate description of Mendelssohn as a
pianist compare Chorley's " Modern German Music," vol. i.
pp. 50, 51.

† All these letters are transcribed *literatim*.

allow you to write me sometimes, and not too seldom; I shall always answer punctually, and it would be a very great treat to me to continue, as it were, a conversation which we were compelled to break off too soon. There is none of my friends in England whose letters give me so quite the feeling of presence as yours do, and as you say you must use a dictionary to read a German letter, I will much rather use it in writing an English one, and put you to the inconvenience of decyphering my imaginary language, which I intend for yours. And now I will not say more on the subject, but let us often hear from each other. Thanks for your ideas on the plan of Dives and Lazarus—be sure that I am fully aware of your kindness in thus discussing the matter with me, instead of leaving it off at once, as I unfortunately experienced it so often; and I thank you more for it than I can well express. After what you say, I see that I have not been able to form an exact idea of what you intend the whole to be; the fact is, that I did not quite understand what part both figures should act in hell or in heaven, because I do not quite understand the part they act on earth—and indeed the true sense of the story itself, as I find it in the Evangile—or is there another source, which you took your notions from? I asked some of my theological friends here, but they knew none.—I only find Dives very rich and Lazarus very poor, and as it cannot be only for his riches that one is burning in hell, while the other must have greater claims to be carried to Abraham's bosom than his poverty alone, it seemed to me as if some very important part of the story was left in blank. Or should Lazarus be taken as an example of a virtuous poor man; the other of the contrary? But then we ought to know or to learn (by the poem) what he *does* or *has done* to deserve the greatest of all rewards; the mere reason (as given in St. Luke) that he suffered want, and that the other has had his share of happiness on earth already, does not seem sufficient to me to give interest to the principal figure of such a poem as that which you intend. Perhaps you have another view of the whole; pray let me know it, and tell me what part you would give to both of them in earth, hell, and heaven. If once delivered of this scruple, I should quite agree with your opinion, and the great beauties you point out I certainly should feel and admire with all my heart. Do not lose patience with me; I am of a rather slow understanding, and can never move forwards until I have quite understood a thing. The best is, that in all such discussions one always draws nearer, not only to the subject, but also to each other. But what is this return of your illness, and the continual complaint of which you write me? You seemed so well and so high in your spirits when we met here. Are you not too busy, and take too little rest? Half an hour's rest or walk may benefit so very much if taken in right time; but I am afraid London is the worst place for thinking of such things, which, however, take always revenge if neglected. And yet it must be possible there also. Am I not talking like an old 'Philister?' I am in earnest, however. Pray give me better news in your next letter; tell me that you are quite recovered, and that you will take care of yourself.

" Of the Moscheles' and Klingemann you do not speak. Do you know whether the first have received my letter two or three months ago, and the other   * letters lately, and how are they? What you say of Miss —— is, I am sorry to say, quite my opinion; and the impression her continental tour has produced upon her seems to me very far from favourable. I always thought every sensible person should only improve by kindness shown to her, and be driven to greater exertions by the expectations and the praises of friends; and I was more sorry than I can express to see in this instance quite the contrary. This and a few other similar experiences I believe to be the causes why I cannot think of my returning to England with so unmixed a pleasure as I should have done otherwise; indeed, I find it difficult to

* Original torn.

make up my mind, whether I should like to go or not, while I would not have hesitated a moment in former years. I had some letters about Musical Festivals at Birmingham and Edinburgh, which made me think over these matters very often last week; and yet I was not able to overcome all my objections, and, much as I wish to see again your country and all my excellent friends there, I fear that I shall rather decline than accept those kind and honouring offers. Does not Moscheles go to the Continent next summer? and when and to which place? If he went to Hamburgh, perhaps could I manage to pay him a visit. What you write of the *Conservatoire* of Paris has surprised me, and I could scarcely believe it, if I had not found the same fault in their execution of Mozart's and Haydn's, which you blame in Beethoven's, works; their extreme vivacity had carried them to over-load the two former masters' compositions, and to hunt for effects and admiration where a conscientious fidelity was required, and nothing more. This was not the case with

Beethoven's symphonies, which they really performed without frivolity and exaggeration; but eight years have elapsed since, and as they most probably wanted to add some new and better effects every year, it must be now the same case as with their predecessors, and then I am afraid they will get tired of them as soon as of the others.   But now good-bye. David sends a thousand wishes, and will write in German one of these days. Schleinitz sends his regards, and talks often of the ' Englishman,' meaning you *par excellence.* Once more adieu.

" Always very truly yours,

" F. MENDELSSOHN BY."

" Leipzig, 21st July, 1840.

"MY DEAR SIR,

" I was not able to write to you until I had made up my mind as to my intended journey to England.   My health was not in a very good state these last two months; the physician wanted to send me to some ' Brunnen' instead of a Musical Festival. I felt weary and uncomfortable, and there were many days when I had quite given up the idea of visiting England this year, and yet I deferred writing a decisive letter from one day to the other. Now, since I have come back from the Festival at Schwerin (where I got your very kind letter by Mr. Werner, whom I saw every day and liked very much), I am so much improved, and my spirits are so high again, that the *medicus* withdrew his opposition, and accordingly I wrote to-day to Birmingham and accepted positively; and now my first question is, how is it with your plans? with your beautiful idea of visiting Milan or Vienna, and crossing over with me and staying some time with us? Do you know that such a prospect would make my whole journey to England look bright and gay? What a pleasant journey we would have together! What a delightful chat from Belgium to Saxony! Pray let me soon hear that you still have the same intentions and adhere to this plan, which would give me such pleasure—and write me that you are not angry for my long silence, which is, indeed, the more inexcusable as your last letters are so friendly, so very welcome, and as I always wanted to thank you for them with all my heart. But this uncertainty would not allow me to write a single letter to England; and now that it is at an end, I have nothing to do but to excuse my former sins. I have also written to Klingemann this morning with the same object in view, and shall do so to the Moscheles'. I hope to find them all in England, and well, and the same kind friends as before. I have thought very often of our Oratorio plan; and although I could not reconcile myself to the idea of introducing Dives and Lazarus, your sketches have given me another idea for the introduction of my favourite plan, which I think is the right one, and which I long to communicate to you, and to hear your opinion of it. But I must do it in person, not in writing, and we must talk it over, not only correspond about it; and, therefore, pray keep much leisure time open for me and for my plans. Perhaps I shall annoy you very much with them, but then you must only accuse your own kindness, which induces me to think you more of an old friend than a new one. As for your opening of the second part, with the verses 31, &c., from Matthew, chap. xxv., it is a glorious idea, and that of course must remain, but 'mündlich, mündlich.'

I was glad to hear that you like Liszt so much; he is such an extraordinary artist. He wrote me that he would probably assist at the Festival at Birmingham; but I hear he has given a concert at Mayence one of these days. Is he to come back to England? and is Molique better, who was so very ill, as I understood? David sends his best regards and wishes: he is in better humour for playing and composing than ever, and his new *concerto* at the Schwerin Festival was capital. I am now finishing the *concerto* for him, of which you recollected the last movement so perfectly. By-the-bye, what an extraordinary memory you must have, to write three subjects of a piece, which

you only heard once, without missing a note!
But I have not altered anything at the end of
the first movement of my Trio, and cannot
make out what might have been the cause
of your thinking so. Did they play it fast
enough? I hope you will like my new
' Lobgesang,' or ' Song of Praise,' which we
performed here at the Festival, and which
they will give at Birmingham on the second
morning. It is a kind of universal thanks-
giving on the words of the last psalm, ' Let
all that hath breath praise God.' The instruments begin it with a symphony of three
movements, but then it will not do ; and the
voices take it up and continue it with
different feelings and words, solos and cho-
ruses, till they all unite again in the same
words. It is rather long, but I think and
hope you will like some parts of it better
than my other things. I will also bring
some other new compositions ; and this leads
me to a question which I also put to Klingemann, and to which I should like to know
your answer and very sincere opinion, as I

shall be guided by it. It is now so long since I have not been heard in public in London, that I should like to arrange a concert for some charitable institution during my stay in September next: it might either be in a church, and there I could only play the organ, or (which I would prefer) in a room, where I could perform my new piano-forte music, a new overture, &c. But the question is, first, whether such a thing is possible in the month of September, when everybody is out of town? then, if such concerts to benevolent purposes are known and liked in your country, and, in short, whether you advise the thing to be done or not? If the two first points are not an objection, I should like the idea; but, as I said, let me be guided by your view of the case. The period of my arrival is not yet quite fixed. If my wife can accompany me on the journey, I intend to be in London soon after the middle of next month; if not, I will only leave Leipzig in the beginning of September, as I know, by ex-perience, how fidgetty I feel without her, even among my best and kindest friends. On our journey home from the 'Norddeutsche Musikfest,' at Schwerin, we passed through Berlin, and spent three very pleasant [days] there. I found my family in excellent health and spirits; and they return your kind re- membrance and wishes with all their heart. And now enough of my bad style and broken English; let me soon hear from you, my dear friend, and believe me always yours

" Very truly,

" FELIX MENDELSSOHN BARTHOLDY."

The projected visit to England, which forms the chief subject of reference in the last letter, was duly accomplished in September, 1840; and Mendelssohn conducted the performance of his " Lobgesang " at the Birmingham Festival. On his return to Leipsic in October, he was accompanied by Moscheles and Chorley. The latter's journal of the tour affords a plea- sant portraiture of both his travelling com- panions—' Moscheles of a humour quaint and ' curious, and more genial than I had at all

' expected from one habitually so calm and
' reserved; Mendelssohn warm and petulant
' about small troubles and hindrances, but
' good-natured to an excess, and *spirituel* and
' cheerful passing common cheerfulness.'

They travelled by way of Ostend and
Cologne, up the Rhine, through Frankfort
and Weimar. The Rhine voyage was especially interesting to Chorley, as Mendelssohn
knew 'all the points of the river like a lover,
' and showed them to me with the eagerness
' of one who has sympathy in his heart.' On
the road to Weimar, Mendelssohn recalled an
amusing episode of his visit there many years
before, as Goethe's guest. The Grand Duchess
having expressed a wish to hear him play, an
intimation was made to him that he had better
call upon the Hof-Marschall; but standing on
his dignity, and probably knowing something of
that functionary's mode of treating musicians,
he declined to do this, expressing at the same
time his readiness to accept a formal invitation
to the court. Such an invitation was at last
sent to him, and he accompanied Madame

von Goethe one Sunday evening to the
Belvidere. On arriving, he was asked his
name by the official in waiting, and on giving
it, was separated from his companion, and led
' through a labyrinth of by-passages to a small
' waiting-room, where cloaks and such ignoble
' wrappings are deposited,' being directed to
wait there until the Hof-Marschall came. After
waiting alone for half an hour, the youth
began to chafe. ' At last, provoked and in-
' dignant, he takes his crush-hat, and rushes
' out. The servants try to hinder him—he
' must not go ; he will be called upon presently ;
' every one will be very much displeased, and
' so forth ; to which no answer, save that go
' he will, and go he does, across the fields, in
' full evening dress, straight to Goethe's house,
' leaving the formal court to stare and wonder
' for their pianoforte player ; a circle having
' been convoked expressly to meet him.'
Mendelssohn went on to say that this pro-
test had the desired effect, and that the
court officials were henceforth instructed
to treat Hummel, who had been accustomed

to similar indignities, with becoming respect.

The week which Chorley spent at Leipsic was one of ceaseless musical entertainment; Mendelssohn and Herr David, first-violinist of the *Gewandhaus* Concerts, vieing with each other in deference and hospitality to their English visitor. One delicate act of attention rendered by Mendelssohn on this occasion is worth special mention. A painful attack of lameness that had confined Chorley to his hotel, had prevented him from enjoying several of the musical treats which he had anticipated. 'I was lying down,' he writes, ' in all the fullness of wretchedness . . . . ' when a little bustle at the door announced ' the arrival of a concert-flugel from Breitkopf ' and Härtel. I shall always think of this ' with emotion. Mendelssohn had sent it, ' and he and Moscheles were coming to make ' their evening's music by the side of my sofa! ' One hardly knows how to take these things ' without seeming extravagant; and I could ' not help running over, in thought, years of

' struggle, and obscurity, and longing, when
' such a visitation would have seemed to me
' a positive faery-dream. . . . Then one's
' mind so strongly and sadly associates with
' its thoughts at such times all who are gone ;
' and I could not but remember what a sym-
' pathy poor Benson would have had in seeing
' my tastes thus ministered to, and without, I
' hope, any obtrusiveness or flattery on my
' part.'

Another entry chronicles an illustration of
the composer's *gaieté de cœur*—trifling enough
in itself, but yet characteristic of the man.
While spending an evening at his house, a
note with a ticket enclosed was put into
Chorley's hand. The note ran thus:

" The Directors of the Leipzig Concerts
beg leave to present to Mr. *Shurely* a ticket
to the Concert of to-morrow." ' Where-
' upon Mendelssohn ran to the pianoforte,
' and began to play the subject from the
' chorus of the " Messiah," "*Surely* he hath
' borne, &c." '

Among other acquaintances which Chorley made on this visit were the composer Schumann, and the accomplished *pianiste* his wife. Her command of the instrument struck Chorley as 'masterly,' although 'perhaps a little want-
' ing in grace and delicacy;' but he was less favourably impressed with her husband's music. The pieces selected were his '"Kreis-
' " leriana,"—fantasy-pieces with that affected
' and Hoffmannish title, and written studies,
' neither songs without words, nor *notturni*,
' nor recitatives in rhythm, but partaking of all
' these natures; exceedingly wild, exceedingly
' clever, with some passages of very sweet
' melody, and some middle work of very fine
' construction; but, after all, clouded, and
' dreamy, and heavy: a sort of answer to the
' spirit of Berlioz talking on the pianoforte.
' Surely music is neither to end nor to stay
' here, else will it become a house for no sane
' man to dwell in !'

Chorley's estimate of Schumann's music was never, I believe, materially modified, though he lived to witness the success which, after the composer's early death, attended the efforts of Madame Schumann to obtain his semi-apotheosis.

At Mendelssohn's house in Leipsic, Chorley was treated with a familiar kindness that won his heart. He was especially charmed with the infantine grace of his host's little boy (now Dr. Karl Mendelssohn), and on the journey home addressed a sonnet to him, which, as well for its own sake as for the gratification which it afforded to the composer, may be appropriately inserted here. It was sent to him, as may be inferred, between the dates of the two succeeding letters.

"TO C. MENDELSSOHN BARTHOLDY.

" Now, while the Night with sad embrace hath kissed
  The earth to silence, save for winds that grieve,
  My heart is counting o'er the things I leave
  With tender watchfulness that none be missed:
  And 'mid the ties which Life will scarce untwist,
  O blooming, bright-haired Boy! thou, too, did'st weave
  A tiny thread—with looks that all believe,
  And gladsome voice. Oh, may it aye resist,
  Merry as now, the harsher tones of Time!
  Thou wilt forget me ere again we meet;

And I am townward bound—to play the mime
'Mid worldly men—perchance myself to cheat :
Fit is it then that one atoning rhyme
So fair a gift of Heaven should simply greet."

The following was received in answer to the first letter written by Chorley after his return :

"Leipzig, 24th Jan., 1841.

" MY DEAR CHORLEY,

" Here comes your knife and speaks : ' How long is it that you left me on F. M. B.'s table ?   And why did he not send me sooner to my lord and master, and why did he not write sooner, and why is he so idle ?'   But then the knife is too sharp, for I was not idle, and I wanted often to write and say a great deal to you ; and very odd it was when I knew you on your way to France, and found the knife with your name reposing so quietly on my writing table.   And you receive another debt of mine with it, the ' Evangelium Nicodemi.'   It was long before I could find out a copy for you, and very brilliant it is not, and looks more like a school grammar than like a

poetical enthusiastic Evangile, which, however, you will find it is, when you have leisure
to look it over.   I hope that may soon be the
case ; and you may then think of our conversation in Belgium on the railroad, and in
different other places, and think of the great
work to which you so kindly and friendly
promised your assistance.   But even if you
find at present no leisure to read it, the look
of it will, I hope, recall your friends in Lur-
genstein's garden to your mind, and will make
you think, if not of my work and music, at
least of me and my wife and children.

" I have now three, and a very pretty,
healthy, good-looking fellow the youngest
is.   My wife has not yet left her room, but is,
thank God, so well, and in so excellent spirits
that I really have passed one of the happiest
weeks since the birth of the little boy.   The
time before such an event is always so serious,
and then I had such a quantity of business,
musical and other, in my head, that I cannot
express how relieved I feel since all is so
happily over.

" My wife joins in best wishes and compliments to you, and hopes to see you soon on so good terms with the youngest as you are with the two other children. Have my best thanks for your very kind and welcome letter, with the news of your stay in Paris, and of all our mutual London friends. They are almost as bad correspondents as I am ; at least, when I take the start I beat them, as I have now completely done since our arrival here. I hope from one day to another to hear from Moscheles and Klingemann, for there were many things in their last accounts which interested me very much, and of which I long to hear more particulars ; as, for instance, the Singing Academy which they were to open, and from which I think much good might be anticipated under the auspices of two such artists. The only drawback seems to me the difficulty for English ladies of moving alone (without servants, gentlemen, and other accompaniments *obligato*), which, however, is almost indispensable for such an undertaking ; and (unless it is to be confined only to the inferior classes) I do not know how this obstacle in England, as well as in France, may be overcomed. And then the second, that men of business should consider music, and the participating of it, as something *not* below their dignity, and that they should have indeed their heads free enough to count the pauses and the sharps and flats. With us, who shut up from twelve to two, as you know, and who have done in shops and counting-houses at seven, the thing is quite different; and then all our girls run about the streets by themselves the whole day long ; and then at night, if there are three or four of them, and an old spinster in the rear, they will roam and fear nothing; or the singing gentle-men will take them home, at which idea every Frenchman's morals would go into violent fits. I am therefore very anxious to know how Moscheles and Benedict will have organised this new undertaking, for all those French essays made by Mr. Mainzer and the others are nothing like our societies. Did you hear something of those while at Paris ? and what is your opinion of them ?   And now I recollect that I am still more in your debt than I thought when I began the letter; that I have not even thanked you yet, in the name of my wife, for that charming little poem which Moscheles sent me the other day, composed partly by him and partly by myself [yourself], for the kind, hearty feeling which it expresses, and the delightful words in which it expresses them.   Have my best and sincerest thanks for it, my dear Chorley, and be sure that we appreciate your friendship to us, as well as we participate of and join in it.   You write me that you began a letter to me in the Rue de la Paix,* and made a poem to my boy; although I fear I must give up the former, I wish you would not force me to do so with the latter, and would send it to me; for if I did not, the boy really would deserve it at your hands; he speaks every day of the ' Engländer,' of 'Onkel Chorley' and 'Onkel Moscheles,' and of 'How do you do.'   Pray let me have it; it

* Chorley was in the habit of staying at the Hotel Canterbury in that street.

would give me such a pleasure, and my wife, who has begun English lessons with a great zeal, would also perhaps be able to understand and enjoy it. And now excuse the prattling letter, and let me soon hear from you, your life, your pursuits, and everything in which you take interest. Our musical news will have been communicated to you by Klingemann, to whom I gave accounts of the concerts, of the battle of Cannæ, in which Mlle. Schloss was Hannibal and Mlle. List Rome, and of everything in the way of art-gossip. But from England I am without musical as well as personal news, and should like to get soon plenty of both. Once more farewell, and think sometimes of yours sincerely,

"FELIX MENDELSSOHN BARTHOLDY."

"Leipzig, 15th March [1841].

"MY DEAR CHORLEY,

"Thank you most heartily for your two amiable letters, which gave me a great treat; and thank you once more for the pretty lines on my little boy, which I read with something

like emotion, thinking of the little fellow's
unconsciousness, and that he was already the
object of my and my friend's best thoughts
and wishes. I like the sonnet in itself very
much. I do not know how it comes that it
has the touch of an impromptu, without any of
its imperfections, and that it conveys to me the
feelings of a traveller musing over poetry or
music, and with his thoughts flowing quietly
along while the carriage does the same. Have
also my thanks for your description of my
overture to the 'Midsummer Night's Dream'
being adapted to the play at Covent Garden.
I had not heard one word of it, and it interested me very much. If you could give
me some more details as to the manner in
which all the fairy scenes are given, and what
and where they have done with their "ma-
chineries," &c., and which melodies they have
taken from my overture to serve as melo-
dramatic or other music, you would greatly
oblige and amuse me. Pray tell me something
more of it when your leisure allows you to
do so. Our season is now drawing to its close;

but the second part of it, from January, was more troublesome and vexatious than ever I found it. Fancy that I have had nineteen concerts since that time, and seven more to come in the next three weeks, not to speak of rehearsals of which we always had *at least* three in a week. Bach's " Passione," with our whole strength, amateurs and musicians, in the Thomas-Church, will make the conclusion. But of all this, David, the bearer of this letter, will give you more and better details. I have had so much to conduct and to perform, that I have neither read nor written in the course of this music-mad winter. Accordingly I have not even read ' Antony and Cleopatra ' through, but was interrupted in the middle of the second act, and will now wait till the spring brings better and more quiet times and spirits. Did you give a look to that odd Evangile, and think of the Belgian railways plan ? I wish you could give me some of your opinions about the undertaking, for I shall certainly carry it into execution if I live, and hope to begin—the sooner the better.

Those news of the Philharmonic which you give me, and which Moscheles' last letters confirm but too much, are really very sad; and I cannot help being sorry for the sinking of a society, which once has done so much good to music and musicians. But if it is true that they give my 'Lobgesang' without waiting for the four new pieces which I made to it, and which I announced months ago to Novello, if they do it in the old version, and without once asking my consent, then shall I certainly withdraw all my good wishes for them, and cry 'Anathema!' or make an Allocution to my orchestra, which the Pope has just done about the Spanish affair, and which will be, no doubt, of the same effect on the Philharmonic Directors as on Espartero. I must conclude this hasty and very bad letter. Excuse a giddy man. My wife and children are perfectly well and happy, thank God; and the first desires her best compliments to you.

" Believe me always yours very truly,

" FELIX MENDELSSOHN BARTHOLDY."

Between the dates of the foregoing letter
and the next which he received from Mendelssohn, Chorley had written and published
his impressions of " Music and Manners in
France and North Germany : a Series of
Travelling Sketches of Art and Society." * In
1839, after attending the Brunswick Festival,
as above mentioned, and making a tour among
the Hartz Mountains, he had spent some time
in Berlin, Leipsic and Dresden ; in the first
making the acquaintance of Spontini, in the
second, of Herr David, in the third, of Herr
Schneider, and under their auspices hearing as much music and as many singers
as the resources of the three cities afforded.
He revisited Paris in the early part of 1840,
and spent a month in diligent attendance at
the Académie, Conservatoire, and Opéra Comique ; and in the autumn of the same year,
after leaving Mendelssohn at Leipsic, he again
visited Berlin, Dresden, and Paris, in order
to complete and revise his impressions. Had
he expended half as much care in the arrange-

* Longman and Co., 1841. 3 vols.

ment as in the collection of his materials, this work might at once have taken rank among the standard literature of the subject which it illustrates; but it was compiled, as his journal admits, with a haste of which the tokens are only too evident in its pages. Passages of solid and trenchant, sometimes brilliant criticism, tedious historical dissertations, lively sketches of scenery and manners, and repetitions of frivolous and ephemeral gossip that occasionally border upon bad taste, are so confusedly mingled in these volumes, that the reader may be forgiven if he fails to discover the real thread of connection which is indicated in their title. Such a thread, nevertheless, is really discoverable; and, however unhappily amalgamated, these impressions of a shrewd and competent observer on the national characteristics of the two leading continental races, as illustrated in the relations of their 'art and society,' their 'music and manners,' thirty years ago, may still be read with interest. The analysis of Meyerbeer's "Robert le Diable"

in chapter iii. of vol. i., and that of George
Sand's literary stand-point, in chapter ii. of
vol. iii., which are coupled as correlative instances of the ' unnatural and ill-proportioned
' union of things religious with things sensual'
then prevalent in France, afford favourable
specimens of Chorley's method. The chapters
devoted to the deep-seated insincerity and
levity which corrupted the professions of literature and art in that country, are striking and
suggestive. The same spirit pervades his censure of the miserable cabals by which the musical world of Germany was torn asunder, for
want of that feeling of nationality which its
political divisions then rendered impossible.
Read by the light of recent events, these observations possess an historical significance which
did not attach to them at the time they were
penned; and in this respect the book may
still hold its place among the class of *mémoires
pour servir*. As a text-book on the subject of
contemporary music in the two countries its
value is more limited; but its salient excel-
lencies may be briefly noticed.

In connection with operatic performances in France, the criticisms of Rossini's "Guillaume Tell" (vol. i. chap. 5) and Meyerbeer's "Huguenots" (vol. i. chap. 7) are, perhaps, the most spirited; while of the chapters on German Music, that on the Brunswick Festival is most noteworthy for its genial sympathy, that on the Berlin Opera for its caustic severity. Among the estimates of individual composers that of Meyerbeer is the most discriminative, his poverty of melody, and the artifice employed to conceal the deficiency, not escaping censure amid the hearty praise accorded to his unapproachable dramatic power, and his skill in the management of chorus and orchestra. The sketches of Berlioz and M. Liszt are among the ablest of the minor criticisms. Of the lighter parts of the book the liveliest is the rhymed letter to a friend (Lady Blessington), giving the following description of Berlin :—

> " A wide white city stretched along the brink
> 　Of the thick Spree—no river, but a sink. . . . .
> 　Houses in ranks and squadrons, each arrayed
> 　In one same uniform of dull parade ;
> 　As if old Fritz (whose shade, methinks, looks down,
> 　A pig-tailed cherub in a false bay-crown,
> 　Simpering, to ape the sneer of keen Voltaire,
> 　The while he hovers heavily in air,)
> 　Had bidden the conscript walls to muster come
> 　By proclamation made at beat of drum."

In a pecuniary point of view " Music and Manners " was very far from being a success ; but it was ' more kindly received, upon the whole,' than its author expected, and attracted a fair share of attention, especially on the Continent, where it probably initiated the reputation which he eventually obtained as the English authority, *par excellence*, on the subject of music.

The following letter from Mendelssohn, written after reading the extracts given by the German reviews of the book, may appropriately conclude the account of it :

" Berlin, 7th Sept. 1841.

" MY DEAR CHORLEY,

" Here is at last a letter (a thanking one) of mine : I ought to have written it long ago. You gave me so much pleasure by your last, occasioned, as you say, by some *Frühlingslied* of mine. But by which? I composed such a heap of them, and every winter the evil will be increased instead of cured. So which do you mean? The one I sent to Klingemann in G, or that in B flat? And what an enormously beautiful phrase you have been writing about your book! I cannot answer to that until I have read the *corpus*, not *delicti*, but *beneficii*, I dare say. Strange enough it is that I have not yet been able to get it, and do not know anything beyond what I saw in almost all the German papers, which I found this spring at a Leipsig coffee-house. There they had translated your fine fluent English in their own hackneyed style, one this bit, and one the other ; and they all like and praised it very much, and gave outlines, as they called it, of the whole; but of course that conveyed only a very limited and weak idea of your work to me, and I long the more to read it by myself in the shape in which it was meant and written. There is a man here who promised to get it and let me have it, but till now he has not kept his promise, and I must not wait with my letter any more for him, else your indignation at my correspondentship will rise to such a pitch. Of a surety, I will think of some Shakespearian songs; but never did it before, and such things must have time with me. Is, then, Adelaide Kemble still in England? My mother told me the other day she was expected, or had appeared, at some concert (I can believe Liszt's) at Frankfurt. What is this? Has she left England again for long time? I hope not. Liszt is anxiously waited for by the Berlin musical world, but if he should again disappoint them, and leave Berlin at his left hand's side (as we call it in German) I for one could not blame him; for indeed one of the extracts of your book, which

I read, and which was a quotation from Burney about Berlin, is up to the present day so dreadfully true, that I almost wish you had not quoted him or I had not read it. I do not recollect the words, but it was something to the purpose that the people here made up for their defects in practising the arts, by their acuteness and correctness in critical observations : so they did at Burney's time, which is some years ago, so they do to-day, and I am sure will do after the same period again. It is in the air, in the sand, in the want of historical bottom which their whole life has, in the want of flowing water, of God knows what, but it is. A shame that I should say so, whom they really receive at present with such a kindness, as to make me think the whole town and the people very fine, even if they were twice as ugly; but I cannot help it, and, with all my gratitude, truth will out in almost every conversation I have, and in every letter I write. Yet do not tell anybody of it; I still think I may be mistaken. All my family is well, and unites in many compliments and wishes to you. I wrote a long account of my occupations, and of the prospects of my Berlin career to Klingemann, and will not repeat it accordingly; but I will repeat that you have given me a true pleasure by your kind letter, that you always do so whenever you write to me, and that I wish and beg you to be a generous correspondent to yours,

" Very truly,

" FELIX MENDELSSOHN BARTHOLDY."

END OF VOL. I.

LONDON: PRINTED BY WILLIAM CLOWES AND SONS, STAMFORD STREET AND CHARING CROSS.

www.ingramcontent.com/pod-product-compliance
Lightning Source LLC
Chambersburg PA
CBHW021748110726
47902CB00006B/1437